TE DUE

Pick-Up Sticks

Pick-Up Sticks

SARAH ELLIS

MARGARET K. McELDERRY BOOKS
New York

Maxwell Macmillan International
NEW YORK   OXFORD   SINGAPORE   SYDNEY

FOR MELANIE

With thanks to Emily Bake-Paterson, who told me
the story of losing her retainer, and to David
January, who enjoys a running joke

Margaret K. McElderry Books
Macmillan Publishing Company
866 Third Avenue
New York, NY 10022

Macmillan Publishing Company is part of the Maxwell Communication Group
of Companies.
Copyright © 1991 by Sarah Ellis
First published 1991 by Douglas & McIntyre, Toronto, Canada
10 9 8 7 6 5 4 3 2
Book designed by Trish Parcell Watts
The text of this book is set in 11 pt. Galliard.

Library of Congress Cataloging-in-Publication Data

Ellis, Sarah.
Pick-up sticks / Sarah Ellis. — 1st U.S. ed.
p.   cm.
Summary: Thirteen-year-old Polly's rebellion against her unmarried, fiercely in-
dependent mother comes to a head when they must find a new apartment.
ISBN 0-689-50550-7
[1. Mothers and daughters—Fiction.   2. Moving, Household—Fiction.]
I. Title.
PZ7.E4758Pi 1992   91-26585
[Fic]—dc20

"(Meet) The Flintstones" by William Hanna, Joseph Barbera and
Hoyt Curtin. Copyright © 1960 & 1967 Barbera-Hanna Music. All
Rights Reserved. Used By Permission.
Printed in Canada

CHAPTER

1

"Polly! Can you go get Lionel? The Neanderthals are smoking in the parking garage again!"

Polly pushed away from the table where she was stamping date-due slips and went to the front desk. "What is it?"

"Smell." Mavis paused in her rapid-fire typing of a library card and gave a loud sniff. "Cigarettes. The Hairies are downstairs smoking again, and any minute now the smoke alarm is going to go off. See if you can get Lionel to go down there and evict them."

Polly squeezed past the loaded book trucks to the janitor's room. The door was closed and covered with a patchwork of notices, posters, and inspirational sayings:

1

"The Serenity Shop: New and Used Crystals"
"Let Go of Hanging On"
"Advanced Rolfing"
"Vivation Therapy (Formerly Integrative Rebirthing)"

A new, hand-printed card hung over the doorknob: "I am on the quest for the nothing that is beyond all something. Please respect my space."

Polly returned to the front desk. "His door's closed, Mavis. I think he's meditating again."

"Lord love a duck. Here, take over, would you? Sorry, Mr. Redmond." Mavis smiled at an old man checking out houseplant books. "I'll just go give them the boot myself."

Polly stamped Mr. Redmond's books and they discussed his red spider mite problem until Mavis returned.

"A quick getaway. Smoke hanging in the air, but not a sign of them. At least we caught it before the alarm. Christmas! Look at the time. We'd better start tidying up." Mavis gave the bell on the desk two hearty dings and bellowed, "Ten minutes to closing." She turned to Polly. "Time to clear up the debris."

Polly pushed a book truck up and down the aisles, retrieving stray books and crumpled potato chip packages. She glanced along the shelves for obvious messes. Something was wedged behind the microwave cookbooks. *Boys and Sex.* She slipped it back into the 600s.

Ding. Ding. The bell rang, and Mavis's carrying voice reached the back of the library. "The library is now closed.

Bring your books to the counter, please." A couple of college students unwound themselves from a study table and began to slowly pack books into their duffel bags. Polly gave the book truck a final push into the workroom, flipped on the telephone answering machine, and put the cover on the typewriter. She enjoyed the neat routine of putting the library to bed.

"So, another day, another dollar." Mavis rolled the tape out of the cash register. "Although not in your case, I guess. How long before we can put you on the payroll?"

"Ten and three-quarter months," said Polly.

"Shish kebab! You're awfully slow getting to fourteen. Couldn't you hurry it up?"

Mavis flicked off the lights and the last straggling student grinned and loped out the front door. Lionel appeared with his vacuum cleaner. "Oh, Lionel, here you are. There's a mess of cigarette butts down in the garage. And we need the meeting room set up for the African Violet Society tomorrow."

Lionel leaned against the doorway and smiled his slow smile. "Mavis, does it ever feel to you like things are more like they are now than they've ever been before?"

Mavis paused in pulling on her boots. "Not in so many words, Lionel, but I'll give it some thought on the way home. Come on, Polly. Good night, Lionel." Mavis closed the back door behind them and then pulled it open again. "Lionel! There's a pan of brownies in the fridge. Help yourself."

Sarah Ellis

Polly heard the whine of a bus coming down the hill. "Bye, Mavis. See you next week." She ran up the alley, dodging the piles of crystallized slush that were the remnant of the winter's only snowfall.

The bus was crowded and steamy and there was a mumbler in the back, so Polly wedged herself up against a pole and concentrated on the transom ads. They were all about things to fight. A visiting space alien would assume that human life is one long war, thought Polly, with battles against illiteracy, kidney disease, stained dentures, and "willful damage to this vehicle." She looked around for aliens. Suddenly, in the cold fluorescent light, *everyone* looked distinctly odd, like Martians or Venusians who had missed one essential lesson on how to pass for Earthlings. She had noticed this before—how one day everyone looks normal, and the next day everyone on the bus and in the school halls and in the library looks like someone in a cult movie. Lionel would, no doubt, have an explanation based on vibrations or lunar rays. She'd bring it up at next Saturday's coffee break.

When Polly got home, Ernie was waiting for her in the front hall. He didn't look like a Martian, but just like his regular self. He was wearing the neon green sweatshirt she had given him for his birthday. Its declaration, LIFE BEGINS AT 40, was a bit distorted over his rounded stomach.

"Hi, Polly. What's up?"

"The sky, Ernie."

4

Ernie gave a laugh that came from right under LIFE BE-
GINS. He liked the same joke every day. "Did you bring me
a code?"

Polly sat down on the stairs and pulled a bent catalog
card from her jeans pocket. "Good one today. Listen: K1A
0G8. It's the Royal Canadian Mint."

"K1A 0G8." Ernie said it slowly, tasting each letter and
number as though it were a poem. He gave a big, satisfied
sigh. "I like that one. It's sort of like K1A 0A2. Remember
K1A 0A2? The prime minister's office?"

"Ernie, I keep telling you. I can only remember one postal
code. My own."

Ernie shook his head. "Too bad. But, Polly, what's the
Royal Canadian Mint? I forgot for a minute."

"It's where they make all the money."

"They *make* money? Come on!" Ernie gave Polly a soft
punch on the shoulder.

"No, honest, they make all the coins and bills there." A
gray-and-white cat galloped around the corner and jumped
into Polly's lap. "Hi, Phoebe." Polly stroked her. "Phoebe
used to work at the Mint. She could tell you all about it."

Ernie wriggled in anticipation. "She did?"

"Yup. She got fired, though."

"How come?"

"Tried to put pictures of cats on all the money."

"Like on the dime? Tried to put a picture of a cat on the
dime?"

"Sure did. But she really got in heck for it."

5

Ernie gave another deep laugh, picked up the cat, and held it up to his face. "You're quite a gal, Phoebe, quite a gal."

Polly stood up. "I'm going to see Mum and do my homework. Catch you later, Ern."

"Catch you later too, Polly."

As Polly climbed the two flights of stairs to her apartment, she heard Ernie chuckling and reciting, "Cats on all the pennies, cats on all the nickels, cats on all the dimes . . ."

As soon as Polly opened the door to the apartment, a wall of opera and garlic hit her. Mum was home early. "Hi! I'm home!" Her greeting was drowned out by the soprano in the living room. In the kitchen a pot of spaghetti sauce was slowly blipping on the stove, decorating the wall with a fine red spray. Polly turned down the heat and wiped the measles off the wall.

She peeked into the living room. Mum was sitting on the couch, her legs tucked up under her, surrounded by newspapers. She was holding a pink Hi-Liter pen and lip-synching to the record. Her hair stood on end the way it did when she ran her fingers through it, and she was still wearing her work overalls.

The soprano took a breath and Polly leaped in. "Hi, Mum."

Mum gave a start, toppling the pile of newspapers onto the floor. "Polly! Is it that time already? Come on over here." She pushed aside more sheets of newspaper and turned down the stereo. Polly perched on the cushion beside her. "How was the library?"

"Fine. Busy. Somebody wanted a book on how to teach dogs to read and wouldn't believe that we didn't have one. Hey, how come you're home so early?"

"I left the studio early to get the newspapers. We've got a challenge on our hands here."

Polly felt a chill. The last time Mum had a challenge on her hands was when she couldn't pay her income tax. "What is it?"

Mum pulled Polly close to her. "We're going to have to move."

"Move? Why?" Polly jerked away.

"Mrs. Protheroe has sold the house."

"What! But there wasn't even a For Sale sign."

"I know. But a realtor was in last week and told her that he had an interested buyer who was prepared to offer some enormous sum."

"Does this person want to live in the whole house?"

"No. He wants to tear it down and build condominiums."

"Tear it down! That's stupid. There's nothing wrong with this house. Anyway, what about Mrs. Protheroe and Ernie? Where are they supposed to live?"

"She tells me that the realtor has found a nice condominium for them out in Burnaby. All new, all on one level."

Polly kicked away the heap of newspapers and slid onto the floor. "Maybe this rich buyer will change his mind."

Mum sighed. "Apparently all the papers are signed. And I guess it was bound to come sooner or later. Mrs. P. is nearly eighty and she's concerned about Ernie. She wants to leave him well provided for. And the house *is* getting to be a worry. Remember the flood last fall?"

"But you fixed it. You fixed it fine."

"It was only a Band-Aid job, Polly. The plumbing needs major work. Anyway," Mum's voice got bright and brisk, "maybe it's time for a change."

Polly undid her jacket, enjoying the angry rip of Velcro. "I *hate* change."

"Oh, Polly." Mum put her hand on Polly's shoulder.

They sat for a moment. A juicy tenor poured his heart out to the soft accompaniment of bubbling spaghetti sauce. Polly looked around, at the cat-scratched armchair, at the gray-and-green swirls of the kitchen linoleum, at the cedar tree outside the window, at the familiar house she had lived in for her whole life. It suddenly looked like a house of cards, that you could knock over and forget. She found herself grabbing the edge of the rug, holding on.

She felt Mum's hand tighten on her shoulder. "Anyway, it's not like we have to be out tomorrow. We have two months notice. And meanwhile, there's spaghetti. The world always looks better after a few carbohydrates."

"Can I phone Vanessa first?"

"Sure."

But there was no answer at Vanessa's. "Oh, I forgot," said Polly, "she's away on some family weekend. A party for her grandmother—not the one who lives with them, another one who's visiting. Bad timing."

After dinner Mum covered the kitchen table with graph paper.

"Do you have to work tonight?" said Polly.

"Afraid so. Mrs. Van Slyke needs her kitchen cupboards pronto."

"Didn't you already do cupboards for her?"

"Yup, and it's only been a couple of years. But now she's tired of the West Coast look. Thank goodness! I had my doubts when she said she wanted a sea gull on every cupboard door. Did you come with me on that installation?"

"I can't remember."

"Oh, you wouldn't have forgotten. The effect was sort of like being in the middle of that horror movie about the revenge of the birds. All those beaks. It was not my finest hour as a stained-glass designer. Anyway, now she tells me she wants something more classical. I have an ominous feeling she means Greek columns. But, one thing about Mrs. Van Slyke, she's a good payer. So if she wants Greek columns, she gets Greek columns. What are you up to this evening?"

"Don't know. Practice a bit, I guess. I might go down later and watch TV with Ernie and Phoebe."

"Okay. By the way, I don't think Mrs. Protheroe has told Ernie yet about selling the house, so you'd better not mention it. He's not a big one for change, either."

9

* * *

Polly took her French horn into the bathroom. It always sounded great in there, big and rich and bright. Always, but not tonight. Tonight it blatted and burbled and one key started to stick. Her winter-chapped lips hurt and the weight of the bell seemed to gouge into her thigh. The scales seemed more than usually boring, and she made stupid mistakes in pieces that she'd known for a year. She heard the voice of Mr. Pereira, the band teacher, saying, "The hardest thing about learning an instrument is when you reach a plateau. But you just have to work your way across it." I haven't reached a plateau, thought Polly, I've reached a pit. She gave one final blat, clanged the horn back into the case, and went downstairs.

Ernie was watching an episode of "The Beverly Hillbillies" on video. He owned videos of lots of old TV shows, and he watched them so often he practically knew them by heart. "Watching" didn't really describe Ernie and TV, though. Polly had never seen anyone participate in television the way Ernie did. He laughed uproariously, commented on all the action, warned the characters about what was to happen, applauded, slapped the chair, held his head in his hands, and generally created his own parallel story. Sometimes, like this evening, he was a lot more interesting and funny than the real show. Polly sat through three episodes of Jed and the family, including loud sing-alongs with the theme song, before she got an attack of the yawns.

Later, in bed, she stretched out and tilted her head back

to look at her stained-glass window, imagining, as always, its colors shining out into the darkness, joining the other lights of the city. She remembered the first time she had seen it. Mum had made it for her fifth birthday. Polly had requested a rainbow, and she had expected the kind of rainbow found on a birthday card—a neat, seven-banded arc. Instead, Mum had used small jewels of deep-colored glass that moved like all the colors of the rainbow, from red at the top to deep violet at the bottom. She remembered coming home from kindergarten, opening the door to her room, and there it was, in place. Later, by herself, she had stood on the bed and licked the cold glass because it looked so much like candy.

A few years ago Mum had asked if she wanted a new window. "That one's from my chunky phase. Besides, don't you want something more, you know, *teenage*?"

"What did you have in mind?"

"Oh, I don't know. Shampoo-bottle motif? Some design involving money?"

"Mitts off my window. I like it just fine."

Polly wondered if they would take the window with them. Surely they wouldn't just leave it there to be torn down with the rest of the house. She looked around her room, not a room at all, really, but a converted walk-in closet. Hardly wider than her bed, with a dresser and a desk built into one end. She had looked at every inch of it a thousand times. It was filled with memories—of wallpaper falling on Mum's head as she tried to paper the ceiling, of lying rigid

11

trying not to waken the bears who lived under the bed, of having a fever and seeing her dresser jump up and float around the room. She wondered if she could pack up those memories, or if they were soaked into the walls and wood and glass. She stared and stared, trying to photograph the details onto her mind until her eyes fell shut.

CHAPTER

2

Polly connected with Vanessa Monday morning in the instrument cupboard of the music room. When she heard Polly's news, Vanessa got right to the heart of the matter. "Will you have to change schools?"

"Cripes!" Polly felt sick. "I never even thought of that."

"Because if you do, I'll have to be an eighth-grade drop out. I absolutely cannot get through the rest of high school without you. You are my . . . What are those doughnutty things they throw to drowning people?"

"Life preservers?"

"Right. You are my life preserver. If I had to face school without you, I would simply shrivel and die. One day they would find me, a dry, rattling shell, all the life sucked out of me by family life education and locker inspection, by the alternating *A* and *B* timetables and computer readiness skills (alias typing), by volleyball and the daisies that Brandi Wimple paints on her toenails. You! You are my only link with sanity. You and the trombone!" Vanessa brandished her trombone on high. "You and my trusty horn are my only hope that this," Vanessa gestured grandly around the room, "is not all there is to life."

Polly grinned. Vanessa tended toward the dramatic, and she also managed to turn most conversations to herself. Sometimes this drove Polly nuts, but on this occasion it felt good. "We haven't started to look for a place yet. Mum highlighted the paper, but everything is way too expensive."

"Yeah, I know. Remember when Granny came to live with us? Mum and Dad thought maybe above the store was too small, so they looked around for a bigger place, but we couldn't afford it. Of course, I had the perfect solution. Send Tony and Gino to some permanent wilderness survival camp. But everyone else said, 'Vanessa can sleep on the Hide-A-Bed.' Story of my life. When do you have to be out?"

"Two months."

"That's lots of time. You don't need to worry yet." Vanessa snapped shut her trombone case and slid it onto a shelf. She looked over her shoulder and lowered her voice. "Polly, I think I've found out where he lives. Rats! There's the bell. Let's do lunch and I'll tell you."

Polly trudged off to homeroom. She didn't need to ask

who "he" was. Last September, September 16 to be precise, Vanessa had fallen in love with Mr. Taylor, their English teacher. It had something to do with an indigo sweater he had worn that day and with a comment that he had put on Vanessa's essay: "Well done, rich use of language." Since that date, all conversations with Vanessa led to the subject of Mr. Taylor.

Sure enough, at lunch, Vanessa had barely ripped the top off her yogurt before she began. "I've actually found out his phone number and address. I owe it all to you!"

"How come?"

"Remember when I found out his first name in the office that day when Ms. Litovsky said, 'Hi, Jim.'?"

"Yeah."

"And you know how he said once that he drove over a bridge to school?"

"I don't remember that."

"Well, he did. So I figured I'd just look up a James Taylor in the phone book who lives over a bridge somewhere. But that was hopeless. Do you know how many Jameses, Jims, and J. Taylors there are?"

Polly made a sympathetic noise and sectioned her orange.

"Ninety-eight J.'s, twenty-two Jameses, seven Jims, and one Jimm with two *m*'s. Then I remembered that you told me once about this book in the library that tells people's jobs, as well as their addresses and phone numbers."

"The city directory. People come in all the time to snoop about their neighbors."

15

"So all I had to do was look up a J. Taylor who's a teacher, who lives in a suburb over a bridge."

"That must have taken hours."

"Yeah, all afternoon, but it was definitely worth it. Because I found it! Look." Vanessa pulled a city map out of her binder. "It's out in Richmond. Here's his street." She pointed gently at a spot on the map. "And listen, here's his phone number: two-seven-four, one-nine-five-two. Know what this means?"

Polly shook her head.

"I can phone him!"

"And talk to him?"

"Are you nutzoid? No! Just phone and see if he has an answering message. Can I do it from your place after school?"

"Sure, but not tonight. I'm going to drop into the library for a couple of hours."

Vanessa grunted. "How can you stand working there all the time? You don't even get paid."

"I've told you. By the time I'm fourteen, I'll have so much experience they'll hire me as a page, for sure. Then I'll get paid. And it's way more fun than working behind some counter pouring Slurpees."

"So, what about tomorrow?"

"For what?"

"The phone call."

"Okay." Polly drained her juice and lobbed the container

into the garbage. "Unless we're house-hunting or something."

"Do you get to go along?"

"*Get* to? I *have* to."

"You're so lucky. When Mum and Dad were looking for a new place, they wouldn't let us come. They said we would scare off the landlords. Of course the monsters *would* scare off normal people, but I get lumped in with them, as usual. Story of my life."

"I don't know. I don't think it's going to be that much fun. If only we had more money."

Vanessa nodded. "I know. Why weren't we born into rich families? I mean, it's all luck, isn't it? Mum and Dad could have owned a bank or something, instead of a hardware store. It wouldn't have done me any harm."

"Right. If we were rich we'd both still be the same unspoiled people we are right now."

"Except we'd have better clothes."

"Oh, yeah, that. We'd be the same unspoiled people we are right now, but we'd look *great*."

A discussion of precisely how great you could look with unlimited money took them right through the lunch hour.

CHAPTER

3

All afternoon Polly tried not to think about having to change schools. But finally, in last period—typing—she let the worries well up. Mr. Winterton was trying something new. He was having them type to music, and he had brought his electronic keyboard to supply the sound.

"As you can tell, I *love* keyboards," he said, switching on a boom-chicka rhythm and playing a few chords. In minutes, lost in his own world of old Beatles songs, he stopped paying attention to the class. Polly abandoned the assigned exercise and let her fingers hit random keys to the strains of "Eleanor Rigby." She thought about a new school.

Pick-Up Sticks

* * *

It would be like September all over again, but worse. Starting high school was scary, but at least she knew most of the people. And she wasn't the only one who had locked her locker combination inside her locker on the second day. Nobody would do that in April or May. And what about band? What were the chances there would be a spare French horn sitting around at some new school? Zilch. She'd probably have to change to the clarinet or something. Maybe she wouldn't even be able to be in the band.

Did you *have* to change schools if you moved? Maybe they would just let you stay. Check facts before panicking, she told herself in a firm reference-librarian's voice. She'd ask in the office after school.

The office seemed empty when Polly walked in, and she was about to sit down and wait when she heard a small whimpering noise from behind the counter. She looked over, and there was the secretary, crouched on the floor beside the photocopier, with the instruction book propped open beside her. She was brandishing a pair of tweezers with one hand and holding a scrap of charred paper in the other. Polly recognized the innards of the machine. It was the same model they had at the library.

"Excuse me," she said.

The secretary looked up with murder in her eyes.

"Maybe I can help. Is that a paper jam?"

19

Sarah Ellis

The secretary's expression changed to abject gratitude. "Yes. This is a new machine and I need these forty-five copies, double-sided, for a meeting at three-thirty. But it keeps jamming and I finally got this burnt one out but now it won't go."

"Let's see," said Polly, pushing through the swinging gates. She crouched down beside the secretary. "Oh, you've just forgotten to press the reset button. It's this green one." Polly demonstrated, and copies began to slide smoothly out of the machine.

The secretary gave a big sigh. "Thanks so much. You really saved my bacon." She looked at Polly and blinked. "Er, can I help you with something?"

"Yes, can you tell me whether I have to change schools if I move?"

"You could talk to the counselor."

"Couldn't you just tell me?"

"I don't really know. You'd better see Miss Anicott. I think she's in her office right now. Just down the hall. And thanks again."

Miss Anicott's door was open. Polly looked in. Miss Anicott was sitting cross-legged in her chair. She was dipping into a big bag of chips.

She glanced up. "Come in," she said in a chip-muffled voice. She held out the bag. "Want some?"

"No thanks," said Polly.

"Good instincts." Miss Anicott unwound her legs. "It's a new flavor, Tex-Mex barbecue." She held up her orange-

Pick-Up Sticks

stained fingers. "Yuck." She dipped her fingers into a glass of water and dried them on a Kleenex. There were two boxes of Kleenex on the desk. Polly wondered if people cried a lot in the counselor's office. Miss Anicott stared at Polly. "Polly Toakley? Grade eight?"

"That's right."

"Phew. Sometimes I can't remember, and it's very embarrassing. What can I do for you?"

"I just want to know if I have to change schools if I move."

"Well, that's a bit tricky. Officially, yes. You're supposed to attend the school in your 'catchment area'—that's school-boardese for neighborhood. But there are loopholes. Do you think you're going to be moving?"

"Maybe."

"Okay. Here's what we can do. The loophole has to do with special programs. What we have to do is convince the Committee on Out-of-Boundaries Attendance that this school offers you a special opportunity that you won't get elsewhere."

Miss Anicott pulled a pad of paper toward her. "So, are you involved in any clubs or activities?"

Miss Anicott's pencil was poised and her voice was eager. She's probably relieved that I'm not pregnant or on drugs, thought Polly. "I play French horn in the band."

"Perfect! Just the thing." Miss Anicott grabbed a pencil and began to scrawl. " 'It would be very disruptive for this young musician to change schools at such a pivotal juncture

21

in her musical education.' There. If it turns out you have to move, just come and see me." Miss Anicott drew two firm lines under what she had written and seemed to re-member her counselor role. "Of course, you can come to see me anytime."

"Okay." Polly stood up. "Thank you."

"You're more than welcome, dear."

As Polly pulled the door shut behind her, she heard the crackle of the potato chip bag.

Polly and Mum approached the evening paper with Hi-Liters poised, but it didn't list any affordable apartments.

"Must be a slow time for rentals," said Mum. "But I'm sure something will turn up. Hey! Here's one for two-thousand-five-hundred a month. It features five appliances. I guess that's fridge, stove, washer, and dryer. But what's the fifth one, do you suppose? Electric can opener? Popcorn popper? Maybe it's one of those lamps for drying your fingernails. And listen to this one. It doesn't say what the rent is. It just says, 'appropriately priced.' I haven't read these ads in years. They're quite a giggle, really. Probably just as well that there's nothing at the moment. I'm pretty strapped for time."

Polly sighed. Sometimes Mum was so good at finding silver linings that she totally ignored the clouds.

The next day Polly forgot about Vanessa's phone plans until she went to her locker after last period. Vanessa was standing there, jiggling from foot to foot. "Don't have to house-hunt? Okay, let's go." She started off down the hall.

"Hey, wait up." Polly's horn case bumped against her legs as she jogged after Vanessa. "We don't need to run."

"I want to phone before he gets home."

"But it's only ten after three. It takes at least half an hour to drive to Richmond, even if he drives like crazy. Besides, he probably hasn't even left the school yet."

"Okay." Vanessa slowed down to a fast walk as they went out the front door of the school. "I sure hope he has an answering machine."

"Are you going to leave a message?"

"No way! I just want to listen to the tape. Maybe I'll find out something."

When they reached Polly's place, there were two men in the front garden. One was spray-painting a neon pink dot onto the sidewalk. The other was standing in the pansy bed, looking through a kind of camera on a tripod.

"Hi," said the painter.

"Hi," said Polly. "What are you doing?"

"We're doing a survey for the new owner."

Survey? What did that mean? "Oh," said Polly. She stood and stared at the man in the pansy bed. He was wearing workmen's boots, and he was standing right on the only flowers left in the winter garden, squashing them into the mud. But of course, they weren't going to care about flowers when they were going to tear the whole house down. Polly felt like punching the man in the stomach.

23

"Come *on*," said Vanessa, pulling at Polly's sleeve.

They went inside. As soon as Vanessa touched the phone, she started to take deep, noisy breaths. "I can't. I'm too nervous."

"Well, okay, we'll do it another day. Want some juice?"

Polly might as well have been talking to a wall. Vanessa took one more deep breath. "But I *must* do it." She dialed slowly and deliberately. She listened for a few seconds and then crashed the receiver down. "Somebody's there!"

"What did they say?"

"Nothing. I hung up when I heard the click."

"But that could be the click of the machine turning on. Here, give it to me, what's the number?"

Vanessa recited the number like someone saying a prayer. Polly dialed and listened. Then she hung up gently.

"What is it? What is it?"

"There was a message, but . . . It's not good news, Vanessa."

"Tell me."

"It says something like, 'Sorry we can't take your call right now. If you would like to leave a message for Jim or Rusty please do so after the tone.' "

Vanessa grabbed the phone and dialed furiously. She listened and then sank back into her chair with a happy sigh. "I don't know what you mean about bad news. I think it's really cute. A dog. Probably a red setter with a name like Rusty. And pretending that you might like to leave a message for the dog. That's so funny. Did you notice that when he said 'Rusty' he got that kind of smiley voice? You know that smiley voice he gets sometimes?"

Polly hadn't noticed the smiley voice of Mr. Taylor, and she could picture Rusty more easily as a gorgeous redhead than as a dog, but this obviously wasn't a time for total honesty. "Hmm," she said encouragingly.

Vanessa was pink with excitement. "I think we should leave a message for the dog. We could disguise our voices. Or maybe we could phone and play a song from a tape. . . ."

Polly nodded. She knew from experience that when Vanessa was off and running, she could go a long distance on a single "hmm."

CHAPTER

4

For the next few weeks it seemed to Polly that there were houses everywhere. Every second book that she shelved at the library seemed to be about home decorating, do-it-yourself plumbing, or some little mouse who finds a home in a pumpkin. In the window of the gift shop at the bus stop there was a set of canisters shaped like old-fashioned houses. On Vanessa's fridge was a crayon drawing by Gino—a strip of blue sky with a many-spoked sun above a little square house with a door, two windows, and a chimney.

One day she came home to find that the real estate paper, full of houses costing half a million dollars, had blown off the porch and all over the yard. It felt good to grab up the pages, rip them into shreds, and stamp them down into the recycling box.

There were houses everywhere, but nowhere to live. In three weeks of looking in the paper, they had found four places that they could afford. Each time Polly had imagined wonderful places. One promised "prvt. entrance." It would be like their own little house. A "2 bdrm" meant she would have her own real bedroom. And the "gdn apt" she had seen as full of wicker furniture and the smell of flowers. But of the four apartments, three were "adults only," and one was already rented by the time they phoned. Mum kept saying, "Don't worry. We'll find something." "Don't worry" started to sound like the stupidest phrase in the world to Polly. Great, we don't have anywhere to live, but at least we're not worried, she silently replied.

Their first real lead came at the dentist's. Polly and Mum had a dual appointment. Dr. Jang gave them a discount when they came together. As usual, Polly rushed Mum into getting there on time, only to have to hang around the waiting room.

"Whoever is in there must be having a root canal or something," said Mum, looking at her watch and tapping her feet on the floor. "Oh well, I guess we should see what's in tonight's paper." She pulled the newspaper out of her backpack and turned to the classifieds.

After a few minutes, she started jabbing her pen at the paper and ranting: "Look what they're asking for a studio, for Pete's sake. Who's going to pay that? Look at this, no pets, no children. They're anti-life, that's what they are. Oh great, here's one in our price range, just a two hour bus ride from the city, that's all."

Mum's voice was getting louder and louder, and Polly saw two metal-mouthed teenage boys across the waiting room smirk at each other.

"Let's see," she said, leaning over the paper, speaking in a low voice and hoping Mum would take the hint. Mum didn't take the hint. She never did take the hint in public.

"My question is, where are non-yuppies supposed to live, anyway?" Mum addressed her question to the room at large. The boys began to giggle.

Polly gave up, moving away from Mum on the couch and holding a brochure on plaque prevention in front of her face.

"Polly?" The thin-lipped receptionist came in, holding Polly's chart. Polly jumped up. Good. Even biting into a trough of revolting fluoride gel was better than being around Mum in public when she got on her high horse about something.

Dr. Jang was his usual hypercheerful self. He breezed into the room, tweaked Polly's nose, and inquired, "What's this, then? A big tooth?" Polly smiled weakly, wondering when Dr. Jang was going to notice that she wasn't seven years old anymore. In the adjoining room she heard Mum's voice, talking to the hygienist.

Polly finished first and sat in the waiting room, looking

at the gory pictures in the first chapter of *Dentistry through the Ages*. She wondered if there would be enough money for the bill this time. A couple of years ago Polly had had orthodontia and Mum was still paying it off. Sometimes there wasn't enough money, and then there would have to be a long talk with the receptionist about when they would be able to pay. Sometimes Dr. Jang bounced by and said, "Why don't you just do me a piece of glass?" and then the receptionist's lips got even thinner. "How would you like me to handle this invoice, then, Doctor?" Polly had heard other kids complaining about going to the dentist because it hurt. Polly hated to go because it was embarrassing.

When the door from the waiting room opened, Mum's voice boomed out, but the talk didn't seem to be about the bill.

"That's terrific. So he's giving his notice at the end of the month? You don't mind if I give him a call? No, it sounds great. Thanks for the lead, Betty. I knew something would turn up. Who would have thought that salvation might lie in the brother-in-law of my dental hygienist?"

Mum came into the waiting room and gave Polly the thumbs-up sign. "Our problems might be solved."

Polly stood up and smiled at Mum, hoping that she would just keep moving—through the waiting room and out the door—before they had to share their good news with everyone. But Mum stopped to put her wallet into her backpack, and as she did so, she started to hum along to the piped-in music.

Polly tried to send an urgent message by ESP. Please don't sing. Just don't sing.

Mum took a deep breath. Polly opened the door. The chorus came around. "Memories . . ." Polly quickly pulled the door shut behind them.

As they waited for the bus, Mum told her the news. "So, Betty's brother-in-law has been transferred, and he's giving notice at the end of the month. She's going to phone him and tell him about us. We can go over and see the place, and if we like it, we can go with him when he gives his notice and be the first people asking for the apartment."

"What's the place like?"

"Well, I didn't get many details. They kept vacuuming my mouth out in the middle of the conversation. But the location is okay. It's a one-bedroom plus den. They do take children and we can just afford it if we're careful."

Don't get happy, said a warning voice in Polly's head. But she couldn't help it. Mum's enthusiasm was catching. She sucked cold air in through her very clean teeth and let herself hope.

The building turned out to be a high rise. Mum buzzed the intercom. "Seventeen-oh-four," she said to Polly. "I wonder if we'll need oxygen." As they waited for the elevator, Polly looked around the lobby. A wall of mirrors reflected a couch and a coffee table. Both were chained to the floor.

Pick-Up Sticks

The dental hygienist's brother-in-law, John, was big and had a square-cut ginger beard. He reminded Polly of someone that she couldn't quite place. When she saw a blue duffel coat hanging in the hall it came to her—Paddington Bear.

It didn't take long to tour the apartment. The living room had beige walls, beige drapes, and beige wall-to-wall carpeting. Polly went over and looked out the window. A pinky-gold sunset was reflected in the windows of the neighboring buildings. Lights began to twinkle on. A man talked on a phone as he walked along the street. A couple took turns pushing a stroller. A dog with a girl at the end of his leash meandered his way from smell to smell along the grass boulevard. Cars took their orderly turns at the four-way stop. It was like a giant dance.

"Well," said Mum in her silver-lining voice, "I'm sure it's nice and bright. And we could put up some leaded-glass panels. Sort of make the place our own."

"I don't know," said John. "They're quite fussy about the outside of the building looking uniform. It says in the lease that you can't change the curtains, for example. They might not go for the window idea."

The bedroom was small and the den was smaller. Both were beige and very neat. Even the closets were tidy. Polly wondered where John kept his junk. The den had louvered sliding doors. When John pulled them shut it made a small, enclosed space. Just like my room at home, thought Polly.

Mum sighed. "It's all a bit monochromatic for my taste,

31

but . . ." She made an obvious effort to perk up. "But you can do wonders with a couple of rolls of wallpaper and some paint."

"Actually," said John, with a shy laugh, "they're pretty strict about paint colors, too. Just the approved ones and no wallpaper."

They stuck their heads into the beige bathroom and walked single file, through the almond-colored, corridor kitchen back to the living room. Mum slid open the glass doors to the balcony. It was wide enough for one skinny person to stand.

"I guess I could keep my bike out there," said Mum.

"Oh, they don't allow bikes on the balconies," said John. "There's a locker downstairs."

Polly saw Mum begin to stiffen. No, please don't say anything, she begged inwardly. It's not his fault.

And, mercifully, Mum contained herself. "Oh," she said in a small voice.

John offered them a cup of tea, and they sat on the couch as he told them about the laundry room and the garbage and the security deposit.

Polly could tell by the way Mum was saying "ah-hum" and not asking questions that she wasn't paying attention, that she had already decided against the apartment.

Mum gulped the last of her tea. "I think Polly and I should talk it over," she said. "Is it all right if I get in touch with you before you give notice?"

"Sure," said John, "I'm not telling anyone else."

Pick-Up Sticks

"Thanks for letting us have a look," said Mum. "And pass along our thanks to Betty, would you?"

"No problem. The rental situation's pretty tight, eh?"

In the elevator Mum held up her scarf and pretended to hang herself. "Aagh! I'm being beige'ed to death. I thought for that amount of rent you'd get something really *swell*. And talk about rules! There's probably something in the lease about which way to unroll your toilet paper. I sure couldn't live there." As the elevator reached the main floor she glanced at Polly. "What about you, honey?"

Polly felt the apartment slipping away. Hot anger bubbled inside her. "Well, what does it matter what I say? You've decided, haven't you?"

Mum walked over to the chained-to-the-floor couch. "Sit down for a minute. You sound pretty upset."

Polly dumped herself down. "Why bother to ask me? You couldn't live there. You just said it."

"I'm sorry. I guess I wasn't letting you have your say. *Did* you like it?"

Suddenly Polly went from thinking the apartment was okay to loving it. "Yes, I liked it a lot."

"You're not just panicking because it's the first place we've been able to look at?"

"*No!*"

"You'd be happy living here?"

"Yes."

Mum was quiet for a few minutes. Then she slapped the couch. "Well, then, let's just do it. I've never thought of myself as the high-rise type, but who says it's forever? And surely they wouldn't object to strippable wallpaper if you took it down before you left. Why not? What do you say? Shall we go tell John now?" Mum slid to the edge of the couch, poised for action. She looked at Polly eagerly.

Polly felt as if Mum were looming over her. *Did* she want to live here? Why didn't Mum's offer make her feel great? The volcano inside was still smoking, about to spill over in angry lava, but now she had no excuse to blow up. One thing was for sure—she couldn't change her mind now. She stood up and pushed her mouth into a smile. "Sure. Thanks, Mum."

In the time it took to get to the seventeenth floor, Mum hatched a plan to try to get the whole building organized for composting.

When they walked back into the apartment, Polly let herself see it as home. Maybe it would be fine. Everything so new and clean. A shower. Her own clothes closet. Maybe she'd buy a shoe bag and some colored plastic hangers.

"That didn't take long," said John with a grin. "I might as well go and give my notice now, then we'll have it settled. The manager's down in one-oh-three, off the lobby."

Mum and Polly sat on the couch while John visited the manager. "I'll just tell him you're here," he said.

"Do I have to come in?" said Polly.

"Er, I guess not," said Mum. "Feeling shy?"

"Sort of," said Polly. But that wasn't it. She just wanted Mum to do it.

The door to 103 opened and John beckoned them.

Polly shrugged off her jacket and picked up two take-out pizza menus from the coffee table. She was carefully comparing the ingredients in the house specials when the manager's door burst open. Mum emerged, slammed the door behind her, and swept across the lobby.

"Come on, Polly." Her voice was tight and cold. Polly jumped up, grabbed her jacket, and hurried after her. She had to jog to keep up.

They reached the bus stop before Mum exploded. "Of all the nerve. It's illegal and he knows it, and he knows that there's not a flipping thing I can do about it."

"But what happened?"

Mum let out a huge sigh, like the air brakes of a bus. "You know the rent John told us?"

"Yes."

"Well, the manager quoted a rent of two hundred and fifty dollars a month more. When I mentioned that the annual increase wasn't due until the fall, he gave me this dirty look and said that this particular suite had fallen behind market rent, and that he was just making the usual adjustment. Then he said, 'Besides, Madam, I'll have no difficulty renting the suite in this market.' Bloody arrogant . . ." Mum squeezed her lips together.

"So we're not renting it, eh?"

"Oh, Polly, we can't possibly afford it at that price."

We could afford it if you had a real job. Polly didn't let the words out. We could afford to live somewhere normal

35

if you dressed properly and went downtown and got a job that pays every month.

All the way home, Mum ranted. From the subject of the apartment manager ("I hate being called 'Madam' "), she moved on to rental housing in general and then to the government and then to corporate greed. Thank goodness the bus wasn't crowded. Polly could tell that the rant was making Mum feel better. Polly's inside lava voice went on its own tirade as she stared out the bus windows. But it didn't make her feel better.

When they got home, Ernie met them in the front hall. "Can you have dinner with us? It's pancakes."

Mrs. Protheroe came through the swinging kitchen door. "Oh, I'm so glad you're here. Ernie made pancake batter, and he got very enthusiastic with the quantity. You haven't eaten, have you?"

"No," said Mum, sliding out of her pack and dumping it on the hall chair. "We've been apartment-hunting and, boy, what a dragon we met. You wouldn't believe it. . . ."

Polly saw Ernie frown and she tugged Mum's sleeve.

"Hang on a minute, Poll. You see, we got this lead on an apartment, but it turned out to be too expensive. . . ."

"I think I'll go watch 'Gilligan's Island.' " Ernie slipped out of the hall.

"Oh." Mum stopped abruptly. "Oh, I blew it, didn't I? Ernie doesn't know yet, right?"

"He knows now," said Polly.

"I'm so sorry. What a dumb thing to do."

36

Pick-Up Sticks

"Well, he had to find out sooner or later," said Mrs. Protheroe. "I guess I shouldn't have put it off so long."

"How about if I go talk to him?" said Mum.

"I'll come, too," said Mrs. Protheroe.

Polly headed upstairs. She hugged the edge where there was no carpet and smashed her toe hard onto each rise. How could anyone be so stupid? Stupid, stupid, stupid, stupid, stupid.

CHAPTER

5

"Vanessa, it doesn't seem to me that wearing a ski mask on a sunny afternoon is going to make you inconspicuous."

Vanessa pulled the bright blue-and-green knitted mask firmly over her head and spoke through the red-rimmed mouth hole. "Inconspicuous—no. Disguised—yes. Even if he's standing right there at his front window, no way will he know that it's me."

"What about me?"

"What do you care? It doesn't matter if Mr. Taylor sees *you.*"

"I guess not. I just feel sort of dumb walking down the street with someone who looks like she's lost her way to the ski slopes."

"You'll live," said Vanessa unsympathetically. "Have you got the map?"

"Yup. It looks like it's three blocks over and then left."

"Aaagh!" Vanessa suddenly grabbed Polly's arm in a desperate grip.

"What?"

"I just thought of this. It's not just his house. It's his whole neighborhood. He could be anywhere around here, doing Saturday stuff. He could be"—Vanessa peered up and down the street—"in the drugstore or the bakery. He could be getting his hair cut. What if he sees us? What will he think?"

"Relax, Vanessa, he'll just think, 'Oh, there's Polly from English eight walking along with a bank robber.' No sweat. Perfectly normal."

Vanessa took a deep breath. "Okay, I'm ready."

As they walked along the street Vanessa kept looking into stores, turning her head from side to side in little darting glances, like some overgrown budgie. At one intersection, a dark-haired man in a wheelchair crossed their path and Vanessa jumped. "Oh, Polly, I thought it was him."

"You're crazy. That guy's in a wheelchair."

"I know. I thought it was him but he'd had an accident."

When they got to Mr. Taylor's block, Vanessa had another attack of nerves. "I can't do it. What if he *does* see you. He'll guess it's me. Let's just go home."

"No way, Vanessa. I didn't take three buses and use up a whole Saturday afternoon to get out here, just to have

39

you chicken out. I'll wait if you like, and you can go alone."

"No." Vanessa grabbed Polly's arm in another tourniquet grip. "I need you."

"Right. Then let's go. Now, the evens are on the other side. Should be about halfway down the block. Want to cross over?"

"No. Stay on this side."

They walked so slowly toward the house that Polly thought she was going to lose her balance at every step. Vanessa stopped behind a convenient tree and pretended to tie her shoelace. Number 1343 was a green version of every other house on the block. A driveway, a carport, one spindly tree. There was no car in the driveway and the blinds were closed.

Polly looked up and down the block. Maybe an old lady would run out of one of the houses screaming for help. Polly would run in and put out the fire that was blazing on her stove. The old lady would say, "I guess I'm too old to be living on my own now. So I'll move into a retirement home, and in gratitude for your bravery, I'll give you this house. And by the way, take my car as well." Polly was just working out a schedule for Mum to drive her to school every day when Vanessa gave a yelp and took off down the block in a sprint.

Polly took one last look at Mr. Taylor's house and then ran after Vanessa, catching up with her at the end of the block. Vanessa had pulled off her ski mask, and her hair was stuck to her head with static electricity. "Did you see it?"

"What?" said Polly.

"The venetian blinds moved."

"I wasn't looking in that direction."

"It was probably him."

"Not necessarily, it could have been a breeze. Or Rusty the dog."

"Oh, I hope so. I mean, I hope not. Oh, Polly, wasn't it just a perfect house? Two-tone venetian blinds. And did you see? In the carport? A man's mountain bike. Know what that means?"

"He likes to cycle?"

"No, it means he's not married. Otherwise there would be two bikes. Poor guy. He'd really like to take cycling holidays, but it's lonely going by himself. And he goes to those singles places, but they're not really his style."

Polly sighed. It was going to be a long bus ride home.

"Overloading this dryer is inefficient and can cause mechanical breakdown." Polly read the tattered sign for the fifth time. Sunday afternoon at the Laundromat. Warm, damp air, the smell of bleach, and the rhythmic click of a zipper in one of the dryers. Even in the middle of a crisis, all the ordinary stuff just went on as usual. Just because the end of the month was looming and they didn't have anywhere to live; just because Mum didn't see *any* FOR RENT

signs when she rode her bike around the city; just because
everyone they knew had sympathy and horror stories but
no leads was no excuse. You still had to do the laundry.

Polly leaned back in her plastic chair and stared at the
multicolored swirl of her drying clothes. She traced one red
pillowcase, tossed up, falling, disappearing for a moment.
Reflected in the dryer door was a man folding sheets. Polly
stared at the reflection with half-closed eyes. The man was
a very precise folder.

Suddenly he dropped the sheet he was folding and came
to stand in front of Polly. He had crisp, black curly hair,
and this time he wore a mustache. He stared deep into
Polly's eyes. "Can it be true? Are you . . . Are you my daughter? You are! I would recognize you anywhere. I've been
looking for you for thirteen years. Finally, my search is over.
Oh, Polly, I want to make up to you for all the years we've
missed." Then he picked up Polly's laundry, and together
they walked out to his sports car and drove to the big, perfect
house that he owned, and he and Mum fell in love all over
again and . . .

Here the fantasy ran into a brick wall. Over the years
Polly had polished and perfected this scene. From one photo
of a dark-haired man with her own ski-jump nose, standing
in front of a motorcycle, and from a few details Mum had
told her, she had created a person that she knew better than
anyone in the world. She had met him many times. Sometimes he walked into the library and recognized her as she
checked out his books, serious books always, in three or

four languages. Sometimes she met him on the beach, walking a dog. Lately he was often standing in front of a beautiful
house, *his* house. Always he knew her. But the fantasies
always ended, because the one thing she couldn't imagine
was Mum married.

The man stopped folding sheets and began to fold diapers.
That was that, then. Another family didn't fit the picture at
all.

Polly sat up and blinked. She glanced at the crowded
notice board beside her. "Baby-sitter wanted." "Computer
for sale." "Have you seen our cockatoo?" "Basement sublet."
Polly jumped up and looked more closely at the notice. Two-
bedroom ground-floor apartment, available April 1, and it
was in their price range. None of the little rip-off telephone
numbers at the bottom of the notice had been taken.

Polly tore off one of the tabs and put it in her pocket.
Her dryer stopped. She went over to check the towels. Still
damp. She was about to feed her last quarter into the machine when she saw a young woman eyeing the notices.
The woman glanced around and then ripped off all the rest
of the basement sublet numbers. Polly felt a rush of anger.
How fast did you have to be? Was the whole city one big
game, where you just grabbed what you could before someone else got it?

Well, if that's the game, thought Polly, then that's what
I'll play. She stuffed the damp laundry into the bag and
took her quarter over to the pay phone. She phoned Mum's
studio.

"Quick," she said, "phone this number. It's a two-bedroom and we can afford it. I'll meet you at home."

When Polly arrived home she draped the damp towels and sheets all over the living room. Mum laughed when she saw the room. "Wow, it's like one of those English country houses where the owners are away on the Riviera and only the loyal old butler and the loyal old cook are there, draping the furniture and lighting fires each day to keep out the damp."

Mum could be immensely irritating. "Mu-um! What about the basement apartment?"

"Oh yes, sorry. The place is still available. The woman sounds pleasant and we can go to see it tonight."

The outside of the house was not promising. A big, dark, dripping fir tree overhung the front path and obscured the view of the porch. The yard was crowded—a soggy couch, a tangle of rusting metal chairs, a toppling pyramid of tires, three old-fashioned radiators.

"The entrance is down the side," said Mum.

They picked their way through dog poo to a brown-painted door. The lower half was scratched and gouged. A cracked plastic buzzer hung from two wires beside the door.

This is like some horror movie, thought Polly, but it's not Halloween. She grabbed Mum's sleeve. "This looks horrible. Let's just go."

Mum shook her head. "We've come this far. It won't do any harm to look." She took off one glove and knocked firmly. A young woman answered the door. She was holding a baby dressed only in a plastic diaper.

"Come on in," she said. "You phoned, right?"

The door opened directly into a small room that was bare and cluttered at the same time. There wasn't much furniture, but the shag carpet was covered with piles of newspapers, toys, and clothing. Right in the center of the room was a saucepan full of something congealed. In the corner glowed a large TV, with the sound turned down. A car silently exploded. At the other end of the room were a sink, stove, and half-sized fridge, all piled high with dirty dishes.

The woman hitched her baby higher on her hip. "Sorry about the mess, eh. I haven't had much time to clean up."

"That's okay," said Mum. "I know what it's like when you've got a little one underfoot."

"So, why don't you just look around," said the woman. "This is the living room and kitchen, the bedrooms and bathroom are back there." She pointed out a curtained door near the TV. "If you got any questions just ask, okay?"

The high windows of one bedroom looked out onto the back end of a truck. The other bedroom had no window at all. By the time they got to the bathroom, with its mildewed walls and rusting tin shower, Polly had closed her mind.

"No bathtub," said Mum in a bleak voice. Polly stared at the purple rubber hippo floating in the sink.

"Cup of coffee?" offered the woman as they silently reentered the living room.

No, no, let's just get out of here, Polly tried to ESP Mum.

"Sure," said Mum, sitting down in a big, greasy armchair. Polly perched on the arm.

"How come you're subletting?" said Mum.

The young woman handed her a cup of coffee. "I'm going home. It just hasn't worked out here. There used to be a backyard where Darwin could play, but the landlord paved it over to make more parking, and then Darwin's dad took off, eh . . ."

The baby sat in the middle of the cluttered floor, chewing a plastic spoon. He had spiky black hair and apple-rosy cheeks. Polly slid down to sit beside him. He chortled, grabbed her arm, and pulled himself up into a tottering stand. In the whole room, he was the only thing that was clean, new, unbroken, and happy. Polly played peekaboo with her scarf. The baby crawled up onto her lap, where he felt surprisingly solid and heavy. Polly blew into her glove to turn it into a balloon, and the baby looked astonished. She did it again, and the baby looked astonished again.

The rhythm of the conversation changed, and Polly tuned in again.

". . . not quite what we were looking for," said Mum.

"I know," said the woman, with a sigh. "Too crummy, eh?"

"Well"—Mum hesitated—"yes."

"I figured," said the woman, scooping up Darwin.

"I hope this doesn't leave you in the lurch," said Mum.

"I don't think the landlord can force you to find someone to take over the lease, anyway."

"No, it's okay. I've had three other calls. I'm sure I'll find someone. I guess the rental market is . . ."

"Pretty tight," said Mum, with a grin. She put her hand on the woman's arm. "I hope everything works out for you and Darwin."

Mum was very quiet on the walk to the bus stop. "Is that what you get for what we can pay?" she muttered. By the time they reached the graffiti-covered bench at the bus stop, she had recovered, however. "I can't believe that a landlord would pave over a yard when he knows there's a child living there. And to make her find new tenants. That's outrageous!"

"So, what are we going to do?" Polly dug her fingernails into the painted bench.

"Keep looking, I guess. After all"—Mum brightened—"we still have a whole month."

Polly clicked her tongue on the roof of her mouth. "We *don't* have a whole month. Everybody who is going to give a month's notice has already done it, days ago. There's not going to be anything new in the paper now."

"Well, I still don't think we need to panic. After all, if worse comes to worst, we could put the furniture in storage and camp out in the studio until we find a place. It could be kind of fun. Remember that week we stayed there when the painters came? We can have that as a backup plan."

Polly sighed. A week living in one room with your mother may be fun when you're nine. The same arrangement when you're thirteen—and it could be for *months*—is a different story. "I don't think so."

Mum suddenly spun around on the bench. "Listen, Polly. I'm starting to find your attitude just a little unhelpful. I know you're tense about this, but we will eventually find somewhere. We're not going to be living on the street. I'm doing my best. If you're mad or worried, say so. But just quit it with this silent business."

Polly felt as if someone had punched her in the stomach. Mum never talked like that. And, anyway, talk about unfair. Who had found that basement, anyway? Where were all the great places that Mum was finding? She turned away, relieved to hear the click of the bus trolley in the distance. Mum didn't like silence? She didn't know what silence was.

CHAPTER

6

Polly practiced her silence on the bus ride home. When they arrived, there was a big silver-gray car pulling into the driveway.

"That looks like Roger's car," said Mum. "What's he doing here?"

Roger was Mum's brother, but he wasn't exactly the dropping-in type. He and Mum didn't get along. Every year Uncle Roger and Aunt Barbie and their daughter, Stephanie, invited them over on Boxing Day, and every year Mum made the same resolution. "This year I'm not going to let him get to me. I'll just eat my cold cuts and thank him nicely for my electric lettuce spinner or my automatic martini shaker. And then he'll open the piece of glass that

I've made for him and that he'll never hang, and then we'll discuss the weather." Every year the resolution failed, and Mum and Roger would end up in a giant argument over nuclear arms or abortion or the Newfoundland seal hunt. Last year the topic had been the food bank, with Uncle Roger maintaining that people wouldn't need it if they just managed their money well and didn't eat at McDonald's. Their words had exploded in the air like fireworks as Aunt Barbie dodged between them, trying to smooth things over with eggnog and fruitcake. The combination of tension and too much dessert usually resulted in Polly's retreating to one of the many bathrooms to throw up.

Between Boxing Days, there wasn't much back-and-forth visiting, and Polly couldn't ever remember Roger arriving unannounced.

He was wearing a camel hair overcoat unbuttoned over his suit, and as he emerged from his car he looked huge. "Hi there," he bellowed, "glad I caught you in."

"Come on up," said Mum. "Have coffee."

Sitting in the living room, filling up the armchair, his legs stretched out, Uncle Roger gave the same impression of overwhelming bigness. He enveloped a coffee mug in one large hand. "So, I dropped over because Barbie told me that you were looking for a place to live."

"Yes, Mrs. Protheroe is selling the house."

"Smart lady. I'd say that real estate is really peaking. Bet she's getting a bundle. H. K. money, is it?"

"What?"

"You know, Hong Kong buyer?"

"I really don't know."

"Anyway, I think I've got a lead for you. There's a fellow in my office, heck of a guy, sales manager for the western region, and he owns this property in the West End. Six stories, twenty-two apartments, that sort of a job. And he needs a residential manager. The deal is free rent and a nominal salary, to be negotiated."

Mum looked wary. "What does the job entail?"

"Some cleaning, vacuuming the halls mostly, showing suites as they become vacant, and then more or less just being there."

"What do you mean, being there?"

"Well, you know, in the day—for deliveries, repairmen, emergencies, things like that."

"But, Roger, I already have a job."

"I know, I know, the glass. But you could do that in your spare time, couldn't you? Weekends?"

"Roger, if you were a contractor and you were building a house and you needed someone to do the leaded-glass skylights, how likely is it that you would choose someone who could only work weekends?"

"You work with contractors?" Roger looked flabber-gasted.

"Did you think I'd been making a living for seventeen years selling stained-glass mushrooms at crafts fairs? Get real, Roger."

"I guess I hadn't thought that much about it."

51

"Right." Mum took a deep breath and Polly jumped in. "What's it like, this apartment?"

"It's a couple of years old. Real nice. Skylights, squash court, pool, and jacuzzi. The whole deal."

A pool? Right in the building. That would be great. Early morning swims, pool parties . . .

"Thanks for keeping me in mind, Rog," said Mum, "but I don't see how I can take advantage of the offer."

Roger pushed himself forward in his chair. "That's too bad. It's a real nice building as I say, well maintained and not too dark."

"Too dark?" said Mum. "Doesn't that depend on the way the windows are facing?"

"Hyuh, hyuh. You're a card, Joanie. No, I was referring to the tenants."

"Oh," said Mum, in an ominous, small voice. A vein in her temple started to throb.

"So, when do you have to be out?"

"April first."

Uncle Roger heaved himself out of the chair. "Gee, coming up on you pretty fast, then."

"We'll manage," said Mum.

"Yeah, well, look. Barbie and me, we're always glad to have you come and stay with us, anytime. Honest. There's the whole basement, your own bathroom, the whole schmear. You know, if you need a place for a month, or whatever."

Mum didn't say anything, and Uncle Roger jumped into

the silent wake of his offer. He patted Polly's shoulder heavily, "So, still playing the trumpet?"

"French horn, but yes. I might be playing a solo at the year-end concert."

Uncle Roger's voice was vague and jovial. "Great, that's just great. So, I better hit the road. Thanks much for the coffee, Joanie, and let us know how you're doing, eh?"

"Okay. Good night, Roger."

Polly walked Uncle Roger downstairs. When they reached the front hall, Ernie popped out of his room. "Hey, Polly, guess what?" Then he saw Uncle Roger and ducked his head down in the shy way he had with strangers.

"Ernie, this is my Uncle Roger. I think you met him once, a few years ago."

"Pleased to meet you," said Ernie, extending his hand but not looking up.

Uncle Roger didn't see the outstretched hand. He laughed nervously. "Good to see you again. Hear you're moving?"

Ernie let his hand fall to his side. "I don't care to talk about that." Then he slid back into his room.

"Well, I'm off," said Uncle Roger, opening the front door. "Talk to you soon."

Polly had the feeling that Mum was going to have a lot to say about the visit, and sure enough, she was crashing dishes into the sink and starting on a major rant. "Of all the arrogant . . . What makes him think . . . Why do I always think it's going to be different? Talk about condescending. 'Why can't I just do my little hobby on weekends?' "

Polly made her voice small and cold. "So, you're not even considering it?"

Mum stopped washing. "What?"

"You're not even going to consider that manager offer?"

"Well, of course not. It's impossible."

"Don't I get an opinion?"

Mum threw the dishcloth into the sink and splashed soapy water up the wall. "Polly, really, even if by some chance I could arrange the time, how could I do that job? Did you hear that remark about keeping the building from getting too dark? Do you know what he meant by that?"

Hot-lava anger filled Polly. "Yes, I know what it means. I knew what it meant as soon as he said it. He's a racist jerk. But you know what? I don't care. Get it? *I don't care!* You're so busy being good. You worry about that lady in the basement apartment. You're always getting upset about what's wrong with the world. Look what's wrong *right here*." Polly reached up and ripped the calendar off the wall. "Have you noticed? We've looked for a whole month, and we haven't even come *close* to finding anywhere to live. Do you think some miracle is going to happen? Are you counting on some fairy godmother?"

Mum started to say something, but Polly spoke over her, the words welling up from deep inside her. "Would it be such a big, hairy disaster to take that manager's job? Other people have real jobs. Other people make enough money.

Other people get married. You're always so big on choosing. 'I chose to be an artist.' 'I chose to be a single mother.' I've heard about that enough times. Well, why did you choose it if you can't even do it right!" A lump rose in Polly's throat, stifling the alien voice. She didn't look at Mum but grabbed her jacket from the railing and ran down the stairs.

"Polly! Wait!"

She jumped down the last few stairs into the front hall and nearly crashed into Ernie. He grinned. "Now I can tell you about . . ."

Polly just shook her head, registering Ernie's surprised, disappointed look as he melted back into his room.

I have to get away, was all she could think of.

When she reached the street she began to run, as hard as she could, enjoying the smash of each step onto the pavement, wanting to break it, or herself. She ran with no destination, until her breath came in short, painful spurts and a jagged pain in her side forced her to slow down. She blinked tears from her eyes and looked to see where she was. Across the street was the park—the swings and see-saws and tennis courts standing damp and deserted in the darkness.

She crossed the street and sat down on one of the swings. She gripped the cold chains and began to pump, jerking her weight forward and back, keeping her mind empty of everything except the image of her swing transcribing an arc on the purple sky. She remembered stories of kids going over the top. She stopped pumping for a moment, and as she did, the world started to tilt—and her stomach with it. She gripped the chains harder, squeezed her eyes shut, and dragged her feet in the dirt, coming to an abrupt stop.

She sat for a moment, letting her head clear and feeling the thick canvas of the swing cutting into her thighs. A group of people were walking toward her across the soccer field. They must have seen her swinging. Suddenly self-conscious, she stood up and walked away, trying to look as though she weren't hurrying. As she walked, she listened to the cold, confident, sarcastic voice in her head talking to Mum, repeating the words, like biting down on a sore tooth, over and over. "Other people get married. But not you; you just say to yourself, 'I'd like a baby,' and you don't even marry the father and you don't even keep in touch with him and then you think you can say, 'Having you was the best decision I ever made' and then it's all fine and wonderful."

You wouldn't be here at all if she hadn't made that decision. The voice of fairness and logic threatened to break in, but there was no room for it.

Polly looked up and found herself at the top of a hill overlooking the city. A carpet of lights, a stretch of black water, and then lights again, creeping halfway up to the mountain. Every one of them a place to live. None of them theirs. One of them Uncle Roger's. With rooms and rooms. Lots of doors to close. Mum would never go there.

She went home via the fire escape, avoiding Ernie. She headed toward her room, but Mum intercepted her in the hall. She put her hand on Polly's arm and looked at her hard. "Polly, we need to talk."

Polly squirmed out of reach and focused her gaze on Mum's left shoulder. "I've got homework."

"Don't you want some dinner first? I've made some leftovers-in-a-frying-pan glop."

Quit being cute. I hate it when you try to be cute. Polly made her voice carefully neutral. "No, thanks. I'm not hungry."

Mum gave a short, sharp sigh and turned toward the kitchen. "Okay. Maybe later."

"Mum?"

"Yes?" Mum spun around and her voice brightened.

"You know that offer of Uncle Roger's? I *would* like to go and stay with him until we find a place."

"Oh." Mum swallowed. "Are you sure?"

"Yeah. I want to."

Mum paused and arranged her face. "That's probably a good idea. Makes sense. Roger and Barbie certainly have the extra room. If nothing comes up, I probably will camp out at the studio, but I guess that's not very convenient for you to get to school. Yes, on the whole I think that's quite a sound decision. When do you think you might go?"

"Well, I've got exams the last two weeks in March. It would be hard to move in the middle of that, so I thought I'd like to go next week."

"Right then, maybe I'll start some packing after dinner."

Mum touched Polly's arm lightly and the conversation fizzled out.

Polly went to her room and flipped through some French homework. She stared at the same irregular verb for five minutes without taking it in. She snapped her binder shut in disgust and took her horn into the bathroom. She began to play scales, long sustained notes, notes she was in control of, notes she could fix if they were out of tune.

7

"Here's your band sweater," said Mum. "Will you need it?"

Polly and Mum were sitting on the floor, surrounded by boxes. "I don't think so," said Polly. "We're not performing until the spring concert, and that's not till the end of May. . . ." She stopped abruptly. Would she still be at Uncle Roger's at the end of May? Sometimes she wanted to change her mind, to jump up and say, "I don't want to be there until May. I don't want to be there at all." But she fought down the panic and said instead, carefully casual, "On second thought, I might." She took the sweater and folded it into the "yes" box.

They went on packing with businesslike efficiency and

politeness, two calm people just getting a job done. Mum started to go through a box of papers—school reports, birthday cards, crafts projects from Brownies.

"I'm sure that's all throwaway," said Polly.

"Probably you're right," said Mum, "but, oh, look at this." Her face went soft as she held up a folded piece of loose-leaf paper. "I'd forgotten this. Listen: 'Oxygin. Oxygin is in the air. Everybody needs it. Fish need it too but they get it from water. This is all I know about oxygin. The end.' Your first essay," said Mum, handing her the paper.

Polly looked up. Did Mum have wet eyes? "Well, I don't think I'm going to need it for reference in the next few months." She tossed it in the "storage" box. Later, she looked up from her sock-sorting to see Mum carefully sliding the essay between two sheets of paper.

That evening Polly and Mum were doing some final organizing and eating Chinese take-out. At least Chinese take-out was sitting on the floor beside them. Neither of them was actually doing much eating.

They had just snapped the last suitcase shut when Uncle Roger arrived to collect Polly, cold air and the smell of cigarettes clinging to his overcoat as he came up the stairs.

"Care for an egg roll?" said Mum, digging out the cold foil container from behind a pile of *National Geographics*.

Uncle Roger looked vaguely disgusted. "No, thanks. We've really got to make tracks here. What a day."

"Jungle out there, is it?" Mum inquired.

Pick-Up Sticks

What's the word for what Mum is being? wondered Polly, consulting her internal thesaurus. Sarcastic? Not really. Snide. That was it. She's being really cheeky and Uncle Roger doesn't even notice.

"Jeez, you got it," he replied. "It's brutal, just brutal. First of all, they're going to sign the deal and then they're not going to sign the deal." Uncle Roger always talked as though you knew who "they" were. "So, Polly, ready to go?"

"Sure," said Polly, standing up. "I'll get my coat."

Mum followed her into the hall. "Polly?"

"Yes."

"Oh, I don't know. Be good or something. I'll miss you."

I'll miss you, too. But she couldn't say it. "I'll be fine, Mum."

"Okay."

They bumped down the stairs with suitcases and bags. Phoebe wove herself through their feet and nearly tripped Uncle Roger. "What the . . . Grab that cat, Polly."

Ernie's door opened, and the strains of "Petticoat Junction" floated out into the hall, followed by Ernie.

Polly put down Phoebe and her suitcase, and hugged him. "Bye, Ern."

"I don't like this. I don't think you should move away."

"We have to. But Mum's still here for a few weeks."

"You're not."

"But we'll visit. Promise. And I'll phone you."

"All right." Ernie slid back into his room.

Curling up on Ernie's couch, watching a little TV, pushing Phoebe around the room in a cardboard box—that would make a good evening.

Uncle Roger cleared his throat. "Have to make tracks, Polly."

Polly felt uncomfortable for the first few minutes in the car. She had never really been alone with Uncle Roger before, without other people and an occasion. But he started to talk on his cellular phone right away, so she didn't have to keep up a conversation. She sank back into the soft leather seat and stared out the window, focusing on the passing streets and then on her own face reflected in the dark glass. Street, face, street, face—she shifted the focus back and forth, straining to see both at once and failing.

The house was empty when they arrived. "Not much of a welcoming committee, I'm afraid," said Uncle Roger. "Barbie is off at some aerobics thing, and Stephanie's at some friend's, I guess. We'll put you downstairs." He hefted Polly's suitcases down the staircase and through the pool-table room to a bedroom that Polly had never seen before.

"So, just make yourself at home. There's a VCR in the pool room. Bathroom's through here. Help yourself to anything in the kitchen. Unfortunately, I've got to go out again and see some clown who can't blow his nose without a form from head office. But the girls should be home soon. Don't bother about the phone. The machine will get it. Okay?"

"Sure," said Polly, "I've got homework."

Polly sat on the edge of the bed and looked around. It

was the most matched room she had ever seen. Curtains, chair covers, throw cushions, sheets, even the towels hanging on the back of the door, all were in the same pattern of red and yellow tulips. They must have bought everything at the same time, thought Polly. Imagine going into a store, walking right past the sale tables, ignoring the displays of seconds, picking out piles of everything, and not caring how much it cost. Coming home, unpacking, throwing out all your old stuff. That must be so great. When she and Mum went shopping, it was usually more of a case of crisis management—replacing underwear that had lost its elastic or the toaster that had blown up. When she and Vanessa went shopping, they had the spirit of true shoppers but seldom the money.

Her suitcases and backpack looked grubby and mismatched, and she pulled open the mirrored doors of the cupboard to push them in. The closet was empty, except for one neat garment bag and some photo albums on a shelf. The dresser drawers, lined with scented paper, were empty, too. There was a phone on a bedside table and a TV in the corner. It was quiet, the silence broken only by the metallic tick of a clock radio.

Polly felt hollow. She wanted to phone home. But that was dumb. What was she supposed to say? I'm surrounded by tulips? I'm probably just hungry, she told herself firmly. Uncle Roger did say I was to help myself to food.

She made her way up the thickly carpeted stairs and into the kitchen. She mooched through all the cupboards, feeling

63

like a burglar. The fridge was a deli dream come true, full of cold cuts, several kinds of cheese, pickles of all sorts, little containers of yogurt, four flavors of bottled juice. Lots of food and nothing that had to be cooked. Polly thought of Blondie comics, with Dagwood Bumstead and his middle-of-the-night sandwiches. This was the perfect opportunity.

She slid one slice out of each of the cold-cut and cheese packages, buttered three slices of bread, and proceeded to glue together a huge triple-decker, using mayonnaise, mustard, and a variety of relishes. She poured a tall glass of milk, set it all on the table, and went in search of something to read. But the only books around were large and glossy, definitely not the sort of thing to prop open while you eat a drippy sandwich too thick for any human mouth. Finally, she found a hardware flyer in a wastepaper basket and settled down to chomp into her sandwich and read about modular garden-hose systems.

Midway through the first bite, she heard the front door open. She thought for one appetite-killing second that it was burglars. She wanted to call out to stop them in their tracks, but her mouth was full of sandwich. And then Stephanie walked into the kitchen.

She was wearing a tight leather skirt, a tank top, glitter stockings, boots, all in black, and huge earrings that brushed her shoulders. She was very pale. "Oh, hello, I'd forgotten you were coming." When she talked, her lips were all loose, giving her a sort of odd English accent. She hadn't had this accent at Christmas. She stared at Polly's sandwich, and

Polly was suddenly self-conscious. Maybe she shouldn't have taken so much. Maybe these were fixings for somebody's lunch tomorrow. Maybe she had made herself too much at home.

"Hi, Steph. Can I make you a sandwich?"

"Oh no," said Stephanie, shuddering so that her earrings swung wildly, "I never eat bread." She reached into the fridge and pulled out a diet cola. She poured it carefully into a glass, leaned against the counter, and lit a cigarette.

"You know, sometimes I think men are absolutely puerile, don't you?"

Polly wasn't exactly sure what *puerile* meant, but it seemed safest to agree. "Yeah, I guess so. Some of them."

"Like, this person I've been seeing. Well, tonight he, like, *reveals* that he really feels I should stop smoking. Then he goes into this whole trip about the big *C* and all that, and I just say to him, 'Look who goes out into the sun.' I just despise the sun. If he's into, like, *changing* me, then it's, like, off. Definitely off. I don't think I'll see him again."

"That's too bad," said Polly, thinking that she had arrived at a crisis time for Stephanie. If this was TV, Stephanie would now admit how hurt and upset she was and Polly would say something sympathetic/funny and they would hug each other and forge a new cousinly relationship.

"Oh," said Stephanie, shrugging until her shoulders bumped her earrings, "it wasn't like, *significant*, or anything." She poured half her drink down the sink and turned to stare out the window, sighing.

The front door opened again and Aunt Barbie appeared. "Great! You made it. And you've found something to eat and you girls are having a good talk. I just know how teenagers like to talk." She pulled off her neon green headband and threw it on the counter.

Stephanie gave a deeper sigh and wandered out of the kitchen without a word. "Stephanie?" said Aunt Barbie, and the cords in her skinny neck stood out for a minute. "Oh well," she laughed, "busy as ever, I guess." She went to the fridge and poured herself a glass of white wine. Then she sat on the floor, splay-legged, stretching first toward one foot and then the other. "I sure had a terrific class. I really don't know where I'd be without Sally. She's my PFC. I mean, talk about strong, stretched, and centered. When I think about how I was starting to let myself go. She saved me."

Polly broached the second half of her sandwich. "What's a PFC?"

"Personal fitness consultant. Silly old Rog thinks she's too expensive, but he really doesn't understand about fine-tuning." Aunt Barbie arranged her legs into a reef knot and took a big gulp of wine. "So, are you finding everything you need, dear?"

"Yes, thanks." Polly drained the last of her milk. "Aunt Barbie?"

Aunt Barbie was breathing in through one nostril and out through the other. "Um-hum?"

"Thanks for inviting me to stay."

Aunt Barbie's look of concentration softened for a minute. "Oh, you're welcome, sweetheart. It will be nice to have another person around. Stephanie and Roger are both so busy these days."

Later, Polly lay in bed, trying to get to sleep, sleep that retreated like a fast-moving ebb tide as she approached. She dozed and then was jerked awake by the sound of the furnace going on. She reached out to touch the wall beside her, but there was no wall. The room was too big. Her nose was stuffy, but she hadn't been able to figure out how to open the window, with its screens and locks.

She reached over and turned on the bedside light. Maybe I'll phone Ernie, she thought. He would still be up, watching TV. But Ernie wasn't happy talking on the phone. It made him nervous. So who's going to help him with his postal code collection? Who's going to keep the Phoebe stories going?

She could feel the questions welling up with tears. She took a deep breath and tamped them both down. If she let herself cry, there might be no stopping. The only thing to do with her mess of feelings was to put them in a drawer and keep it closed. She bashed her pillow into shape, flicked off the light firmly, and flopped back, listening to the clock radio ticking time away.

CHAPTER

8

The X-Acto knife slipped and Polly cut off Wayne Gretz-ky's nose. It didn't matter. She probably had too many profiles, anyway. What she needed were some face fronts with uncomplicated hair. Bending close to the magazine and using the very tip of the knife, she removed the eyeballs from the face of a bald businessman selling fax machines. Then she cut around the edge of his face. Wetting the end of her finger, she removed him from the page. It was important to do it perfectly.

"I must prepare a face to meet the faces that I meet." Polly looked again at the quotation pinned to the bulletin board above her desk. "Just react! Respond!" Mr. Taylor had said as he wrote the quotation on the blackboard. "And bring me a record of your response by the end of the month."

Polly was responding with a mask, a collage of eyeless faces carefully glued onto a large mask-shaped piece of cardboard. A face of faces. She scanned the magazine for group shots. She needed some tiny faces for eyebrows. This was perfect. A crowd scene at a baseball game.

The pinging of the dryer in the next room was like a sound coming from outer space. Polly glanced up at the clock. Could forty-five minutes be up already? When she was working on the mask, time seemed to disappear. Time and all the voices in her head.

She unwound her legs from the chair and went into the laundry room. She opened the dryer and checked on a pair of jeans and a sweatshirt. Still a bit damp. She set the timer for ten more minutes and leaned against the dryer's warm side. At Uncle Roger's you could have all your clothes clean at the same time. You didn't need to plan ahead to save your favorite shirt. You didn't need to wait for a full load of lights and whites. Polly did laundry every night.

Life at Uncle Roger's was so easy. No lugging her horn to school in the rain. Uncle Roger drove her. No busing home from the library. Aunt Barbie came to pick her up. No dishes. Just stow them in the dishwasher. No cleaning out the bathtub. Mrs. Clemens came in on Fridays. If you phoned somebody and the line was busy, you didn't even need to dial again; you just pressed the redial button.

You hardly even needed to talk. The family didn't eat

together unless Uncle Roger and Aunt Barbie had a dinner party. When Uncle Roger drove Polly to school he listened to sales motivation tapes. The house was often empty, the only life the little blinking lights of machines—microwave oven, VCR, telephone answering machine, CD player.

Even when the family did cross paths, they didn't have conversations. Aunt Barbie did talk, describing to Polly the disastrous mix-ups that happened at the fashion import business where she worked, impersonating irate customers. But when she tried to tell the same stories to Uncle Roger, he always began to hum tunelessly after about a minute, and Stephanie just stared with her dead-eye look.

Polly checked the digital clock on the dryer. Another hour working on the mask, some TV, and she might go to bed. Not much of a Friday night, but in spite of not having much to do, she seemed to be getting tired earlier and earlier.

There was a low purr from her room. The phone. Probably Mum. She phoned every night from the studio where she was now living. She usually babbled on about some co-op housing group she had found. "It was started by the tenants of an old brick apartment building that's for sale. They need some people to join them to buy the building cooperatively. Of course, it's a lot of work, actually forming the co-op, getting funding, and all that, and the building needs renovating, but it's wonderful to think of a way of escaping that whole landlord-tenant thing."

It didn't sound wonderful to Polly. It sounded like some

old hippie commune idea. Besides, she wasn't going to let herself get hopeful again. If you didn't let yourself go up, then there was nowhere to crash down from. The phone purred again.

If it was Mum, she would bug her again about going to one of the co-op meetings. Polly felt like ignoring the phone. But then the answering machine would click in, and she'd have to phone back, anyway. She ran to her room and grabbed the receiver.

"Do you think I could get away with not learning about the *imparfait* if I just memorized a bunch of weird phrases in French?"

"Vanessa, how did you know it was me?"

"Well, you're the only one there who answers the phone without making you listen to that message first." It was true. Uncle Roger and Aunt Barbie screened all their calls. Nothing came into their house uninvited, not even voices.

"So, are we studying for the French test?"

"I guess so." Polly had forgotten. Since she moved to Uncle Roger's, things didn't seem to stick in her head.

"Shall I come over there?"

Polly hesitated. Whenever Vanessa came to Uncle Roger's she spent a lot of time admiring. "Your own bathroom. Just imagine, you don't have to share a bathroom with little boys who leave Funslime in the sink and don't even bother to shoot straight. And a TV in your room! This is *it*, Polly, this is enlightenment." After the first couple of visits, Vanessa's enthusiasm started to irk Polly. It *was* wonderful at Uncle Roger's, but she wished that Vanessa wouldn't keep bouncing at her about it.

"Nah, I'll come over to your place this time."

"Okay." Vanessa sounded a bit disappointed. "We'll have to use the stockroom, though. Gino's having his piano lesson."

When Polly went upstairs she found Aunt Barbie on the phone in the kitchen. "No, I'd better pop over. I don't mind a bit. Just hang in till I arrive and we'll get on the fax." Aunt Barbie hung up the phone and smiled. "Oh, hi, Polly. Crisis at work. A whole shipment of Marek Vitoni sweaters held up at customs, and the buyer is having a kitten. I'd better go sort it out." Her voice was light and bouncy, like someone describing holiday plans.

"I was just off to Vanessa's."

"Hang on a minute while I freshen up, then I'll drop you on my way."

The hardware store had a mezzanine along the back that was used as a stockroom. A sliding window looked down onto the store, and a beat-up old metal desk, piled high with papers, sat in front of the window. It was a good place to spy on people. Once, when Polly and Vanessa were little, they had seen a man slip a screwdriver into his jacket pocket. They had tiptoed down the rickety stairs and whispered to Vanessa's father, who caught the man. For weeks they had felt like detectives and had spent every afternoon on surveillance. But they never saw another shoplifter, and it got boring. Recently they had used the stockroom as a quiet place to do homework or just talk.

Vanessa pulled a couple of stools up to the desk and cleared a space. "Okay, here's my theory. If I learn just enough off-the-wall vocabulary, Mme. Guerin will be so impressed that she won't notice that I don't know anything about verbs."

"Wouldn't it be easier to just learn the verbs?"

"I can't," Vanessa wailed. "I just don't get it. All I can do is memorize. If I try to understand it, it makes my brain sore." She dug out a piece of paper and handed it to Polly. "Here. Ask me these."

"Okay. 'All out at the elbows.' "

"*Toutes troué aux coudes.*"

"Good. How about 'to cut one's coat according to one's cloth.' "

"Hang on." Vanessa bit her fingernails. "Got it! *Subordonner ses dépenses à son revenu.*"

"Where did you find these weird phrases, anyway? 'To quarrel with one's bread and butter.' I don't even know what that means in English."

"Who cares? Don't tell me, don't tell me . . ."

Polly swallowed a yawn and glanced down into the store. "Vanessa! Look!"

There, standing in the paint aisle and talking to Vanessa's father, was Mr. Taylor.

Vanessa gasped. "What's he doing here?"

"Buying paint, I guess," said Polly. "Wonder why he's . . ."

"Shhh," said Vanessa. She leaned across the desk and slid open the window.

"Do you want to go down there?" said Polly.

"No. Shhh." Vanessa slipped around to the side of the desk and crouched down, peeking over the windowsill.

Mr. Taylor was asking Mr. Martinelli about rollers. "You're sure these will work with an oil-based paint?"

"I'm sure. In fact, I've used them myself." Mr. Martinelli was friendly, but brisk.

"I'll have a couple, then." They crossed the store to the cash desk.

Mr. Taylor reached into his pocket and brought out his checkbook. "Oh, would you look at that. I've used up the last of my checks. Rusty!" He called across the store and a red-haired woman in a leather jacket came around the corner from the electrical aisle.

Vanessa gave a tiny gasp.

Mr. Taylor laid his hand on the woman's arm. "Do you have a check with you?"

The woman shrugged. "I didn't bring my purse."

"Well, naughty us," said Mr. Taylor. "Still, I don't imagine that it's a problem. I'll just use this." He reached over and took a paper bag from a pile on the counter and began to write on it.

"I'm afraid we couldn't accept that," said Mr. Martinelli.

"No, no, it's no problem." Mr. Taylor flicked his hand

in the air. "Most people don't realize it, but any piece of paper can function as a check. It's perfectly legal."

"That may be," said Mr. Martinelli quietly, "but we just couldn't accept it."

"Oh, come on." Mr. Taylor grinned. "Isn't this an honest face?"

Mr. Martinelli shook his head. "Sorry, sir."

"Oh, well, then," said Mr. Taylor, throwing the rollers on the counter, "if you're going to be so . . . rigid, I guess we'll go elsewhere. Come on, Rusty. These folks don't want our business."

As he turned to leave he glanced up to the office window. Vanessa gave a squeak and ducked down. Her chin cracked on the windowsill. Polly stepped back and watched Mr. Taylor and Rusty sweep out of the store.

Vanessa was slumped with her back against the wall, spitting into a Kleenex. There was blood.

"Vanessa, what's wrong?"

"Bit my tongue." She punched a packing case beside her. "What a jerk."

Polly slid down to sit beside her. "Yeah." She crooked her little finger in the air. "Come on, Rusty."

Vanessa turned to her, frowning. "What?"

"You know. 'Isn't this face so cute that you want to just *give* me the paint rollers?' "

"What are you talking about?" Vanessa's face was turning red.

"Mr. Taylor, of course. What a jerk he turned out to be."

"*Not him*. My dad. How could he do that?"

"Vanessa. Come on. Mr. Taylor was being an idiot down there."

"He was not! You probably *can* write a check on a paper bag. Oh, what if he finds out that that was my dad? I'd die."

"I don't believe I'm hearing this. Look, Vanessa, I know you have a crush on him, but . . ."

"I *don't have a crush*. I *love* him. I thought you understood, but you're just like everybody else."

"Well, don't get mad at me. I'm not the one insulting your father and behaving like some five-year-old brat." Polly would have grabbed the words back if she could have, but there they hung, in the air between them.

Vanessa stood up and reached for her books.

"Hey, Nessa, I'm sorry." Polly reached out to touch Vanessa's arm. But Vanessa moved jerkily away, dumped her books into her bag, and clumped down the stairs.

Polly turned and leaned her head against the small back window. She looked into the yard below. Tony was lying on his stomach playing with a set of pick-up sticks. He arranged them carefully in his fist and then gently released them. They fell into a rainbow-colored pattern on the grass. Polly remembered doing that when she was little, making patterns, arranging the sticks into families. Sometimes she had even played the real pick-up sticks game. She had played it with Vanessa. The stick flower blurred.

Pick-Up Sticks

Who was the only girl in grade five who didn't laugh when you plucked out all your eyebrows?

But you'd have to be really stupid to still like Mr. Taylor after *that*.

Remember when you melted her Barbie doll's hair with the hair dryer and she didn't get mad?

Well, it *is* a crush.

Oh, shut up, Polly said to the voices. She stuffed her books into her bag. Being friends used to be easier. Why did things have to *change*? She wanted to go home. Home, not Uncle Roger's. She needed to talk to Ernie. In person.

As Polly walked up the path to the house, she noticed that the daffodils were out under the cedar tree. The thought of them being ripped up by a bulldozer made her angry to her fingertips. She looked up at the windows of the top floor. She had never properly said good-bye; she had just gone away. Before she saw Ernie, she had to do that. She climbed the fire escape and let herself in with the key that she still kept in her key case.

The draft from the closing door sent dust bunnies swirling into the corners. Polly's footsteps echoed down the carpetless hall. In the living room, ghost outlines framed the picture hooks on the wall, and the uncovered windows were black holes into the night. A dying fly buzzed and spun on the windowsill.

Polly leaned in the doorway and furnished the room.

77

Couch, fat chair, wicker chair, bookcase, chest. How had there been room for it all? It looked so small.

The bare bulb hanging in the middle of the kitchen revealed the worn place in the linoleum and the chips and cracks on the counter. The fridge stood open and unplugged, giving off a faint smell of old ice-cube trays. The drip on the end of the tap filled, dropped, and filled again.

Polly hesitated at the door of her own room. It felt as though she would look in and see herself sitting cross-legged on the bed playing her horn or at her desk doing homework. The Polly from before.

But it was just an empty closet. There was a piece of plywood over the window. Mum had removed the rainbow panel, then. Polly gulped down her gratitude.

She walked around the rooms one more time, touching things and trying to press them onto her mind.

Then she went downstairs. Ernie met her at the bottom. "Polly! Are you living upstairs again?"

Polly hugged his big softness. "No, Ernie, I was just visiting. Going to invite me in?"

"Oh, okay," said Ernie, opening the door to the sitting room. "I don't like this visiting. I like it when you live here."

One end of the room was filled with packing cases. Polly sat down on the couch. "I know, Ernie, I don't like it much, either. If only . . . I don't know, if only Mum had enough money to just buy this house."

"Yeah," said Ernie, plunking down beside her. They were both quiet for a few seconds. Then Ernie sat for-

78

ward abruptly. "Polly! What about K1A 0G8!"

"What's that?"

"The Mint. You know, the Royal Canadian Mint!"

"But what about it?"

"Don't you get it? They make money. We could just write them a letter, easy because we know their postal code, and we could ask them to send us money, just enough so that you could buy this house."

"Oh, Ernie." Polly felt love wash over her as she looked into Ernie's eager, grown-up child face. "It doesn't work that way."

"Why not? Are they mean guys there?"

Polly realized that she actually didn't know why not. Why *couldn't* the government just print more money? Obviously, not just for ordinary people. Then everyone would want it. But for the things the government said they couldn't afford. "No, they're not mean. It's just a rule."

"Who said?"

"Probably the prime minister."

"Oh, well then," said Ernie. "He's the boss, right?" He slumped back onto the couch.

This was no way to say good-bye to Ernie. Polly searched her mind and then remembered the gossip magazines in the staff room at the library. She had browsed through a recent article called "Homes of the Glitterati."

"Hey, Ernie, I think Phoebe is going to like it in the condominium."

"I don't like to talk about that." Ernie turned away.

"No, but listen, you've got to because I've got to warn you about something."

"What?" said Ernie sullenly.

"Well, you might not realize this, but lots of jazzy people live in condominiums. Movie stars, people like that."

"They do?" Ernie turned around again.

"Yup. And you know how Phoebe loves those types."

"She sure does. She likes all those people, with their big cars and jewels."

"Right. You've got it. Those are just the people who live in condominiums. They call them *condos*. Phoebe's probably out in the alley right now telling Daisy and Melba and that tough ginger cat from the corner store all about it. She's probably saying, 'Oh yes, dahling, we've picked out this dishy condo. It's the only way to go, rahly.' "

"What else?"

"It could really be a problem if Phoebe starts having those condo parties, with stretch limos pulling up to the door. You'd have to hire security guards to make sure no trashy cats crash the parties."

"Trashy cats with fleas?"

"That's it. Nobody allowed in without a flea collar."

"Would they all have diamonds on their flea collars?"

"Absolutely. But here's what I'm worried about. You've got to make sure Phoebe doesn't get in with those cats who use"—Polly lowered her voice to a whisper—"catnip."

Ernie giggled loudly. "Okay, I'll keep my eye on her."

"And I'll come and visit to make sure, okay?"

"Okay, Polly. You come and visit." A worried look flashed across Ernie's face. "Will you know how to get there?"

"For sure. You'll know your new postal code, won't you?"

"Yes."

"Then I'll know exactly where to come." Polly squeezed Ernie's arm. "So long, old sock, old bean."

CHAPTER

9

"Do I have to come?" Polly tucked the phone receiver between her ear and her shoulder and flipped through a *Macleans* magazine. Nostrils, nostrils . . . A pair of shadowy faces in a life insurance ad. Perfect. She picked up the X-Acto knife.

"Polly, we've been through this several times." Mum's voice in Polly's ear was as irritating as a mosquito's whine. "The whole idea of a co-op is that everyone participates. Kids are equal partners. Everyone is starting to wonder if I *have* a daughter."

Kids are equal partners. Polly mouthed the words into the phone and conducted with one hand in the air. "Yeah, but do you mean I *have* to come?"

Pick-Up Sticks

There was a moment's silence on Mum's end. "That's exactly what I mean. I'll pick you up at six-thirty tomorrow."

The next evening, Polly was sitting in the perfectly clean and tidy kitchen, eating microwave heat-in-a-bag cannelloni with Aunt Barbie, when the doorbell rang. She jumped up. "That'll be Mum."

"Hi, there." Mum stepped into the hall, dripping from the bottom of her plastic rain poncho and holding a sodden umbrella. "It's teeming out there."

Polly opened the hall cupboard to the umbrella stand.

"Hey, what's that?" said Mum, pointing at a dial on the cupboard wall.

"Security system," said Polly. "It's new."

"Good grief," said Mum, "that's what it does to you, owning all this stuff. You have to turn your home into a jail."

"Shhh," said Polly, looking toward the kitchen. She had actually had the same thought when turning on and off the security system, but she sure wasn't going to tell Mum that. She shrugged. "We lock our door. What's the big diff?"

Mum paused and nodded. "I guess you're right. You know, when I was a little girl we never locked our front door. I remember once we went on a driving holiday to Montreal, and we left our front door unlocked. Father said, 'What if somebody comes along and needs to stay?' Of course, that was a small town."

Usually Polly liked stories of the prairie town where Mum grew up, stories of swimming in the slough and running away to the coulees. Tonight she wasn't in the mood. "I know," she said in a bored voice.

Aunt Barbie appeared on the stairs. "Hello, Joan. What an awful night to be out. Coffee?"

"Hi, Barbie. How are you doing? No time for coffee, I'm afraid."

"Oh, I wish I could take you to your meeting, but Roger's not home and Stephanie's taken my car."

"That's all right, we'll manage. See you later. Come on, Polly."

The co-op meeting was held in a church basement. The bus connections were bad, and Mum and Polly arrived late. They hurried down the stairs and slipped into a circle of olive green, plastic stacking chairs. Everyone smiled at Mum, and those close to her reached over to shake her hand or pat her shoulder. Oh no, thought Polly, it's one of those touchy-feely groups. She stiffened and avoided anyone's eye.

Instead she looked around the big, echoing, coldly lit room. Inspirational posters masking-taped to the mustard walls advised sharing and caring. The library meeting room was a lot cozier than this. The group should meet there. She squelched the thought. She *wasn't* going to get sucked into all this.

The group was discussing going to the city council with their co-op idea and how some big company wanted to buy the apartment and tear it down and build condominiums. Everybody was getting very emotional, but Polly couldn't understand what they were talking about. She typed the inspirational messages from the posters onto her knees and then with her left hand played up and down the chromatic scale on the French horn as quickly as possible.

She studied the faces around the circle. One bald man with a beard looked like the puppet that had been Hansel and Gretel's father in the Christmas puppet show at the library. Polly looked around the circle again. *Everyone* started to look like hand puppets. Heads of hair—black, blond, brown, gray, one green; long, short, curly, straight, thick, thin, absent. Faces decorated with eyes, noses turning up and down, ears, earrings, lipstick, glasses, one hearing aid, chins, double chins, beards, mustaches, eyebrows, cheek-bones, Adam's apples. Necklaces, turtlenecks, V necks, crewnecks, boat necks, scarf-at-the-neck. And all of their little arms and hands gesturing and their little mouths opening and closing.

Polly was so engrossed by her puppet vision that she jumped when a boy appeared in front of her. It was the boy with green punk hair. He handed her a bright pink flyer. She glanced at it. "Fight the condominium blight." "Don't tear down. Fix up." Blabbedy-blab. She folded the paper several times and stuffed it into her pocket. Then the man next to her passed her a paper bag. Polly reached into it and pulled out a button decorated with lace, sequins, and a picture of a kitten saying, "Save Mowbray Court." She dropped it back into the bag and passed it along to Mum.

There was lengthy discussion about the wording of the

Sarah Ellis

flyer, and then the group broke for coffee. People kept coming up to Polly, introducing themselves, and saying how great it was to see her. They all had soppy smiles, and they all stood too close.

"Mum. Mum!" Polly managed to lure Mum away from a conversation with the mother of toddlers. "Can I go now? I can get back to Uncle Roger's on my own."

Mum stared at Polly. Her mouth had hard lines around it. "No, Polly, you can't." Polly turned and went and plunked herself back into her seat.

After the break the group discussed pet policy. Polly tuned in and out and consulted her watch. One hour and seventeen minutes were spent on pet policy. Polly was taking her own pulse and trying to see if she could vary its rate by thinking of scary things when the group finally broke up.

A couple in matching sweaters were driving in Polly's direction and offered her a ride to Uncle Roger's. She was relieved to accept. Mum had that time-for-a-little-talk look in her eyes, and Polly couldn't face it.

Back at Uncle Roger's, Polly was surprised to find her aunt and uncle having a drink in the family room. She had never seen them together, just sitting and talking.

"Come in and talk to us." Aunt Barbie waved a hand at her. She had changed her clothes. Her cerise nail polish was the exact shade of the flowers on her silky jumpsuit. "So, how was your meeting? You're such a little gal-on-the-go, isn't she, Rog? Turn the TV down, would you, honey?"

Uncle Roger grunted and trained his zapper toward the

86

TV. Aunt Barbie gave a sharp-edged little laugh. Polly wondered if they had been fighting. There was a kind of crackling tension in the room.

"The meeting was okay."

Uncle Roger turned his recliner toward her. "What was it all about?"

Polly began to describe the plans of the co-op, as much as she understood them. Halfway through her description, Uncle Roger began to hum quietly, and his eyes strayed toward the TV.

"Anyway," said Polly, yawning, "I think I'll go to bed. I'm pretty tired."

"Oh, don't go," said Aunt Barbie. There was a pleading tone in her voice. "Tell us some more. Who are the people in the group?"

Polly thought of the puppets. "Well, the chairman is this guy with really thick, wavy hair and one of those jaws. You know the kind, like on the covers of Heart-Throb romances?"

Aunt Barbie giggled and nodded. Uncle Roger stopped humming.

"And then there was a couple in matching sweaters."

"His and Hers?" squeaked Aunt Barbie. "How wonderfully retro."

". . . and an old lady in an orange-and-purple crocheted hat that looked just like a tea cozy."

Uncle Roger was grinning, and he ran his fingers through his hair and looked for a second just like Mum. "Typical, just typical. Waifs, strays, and misfits. Joan just attracts them. Always has."

Into Polly's head flashed an image of Ernie, shoveling snow and singing the theme from "The Mary Tyler Moore Show." She pushed it firmly away. It felt so great to be entertaining Uncle Roger and Aunt Barbie. She wasn't tired anymore. It was as if somebody had pressed her reset button.

Uncle Roger tipped one notch farther back in his lounger. "What sort of things do they discuss, anyway?"

"Well, tonight they mostly talked about pets. There was something about only two pets per apartment, and then somebody says, 'What about guppies?' so somebody else says, 'Okay, two uncaged pets per apartment,' and then Mr. Guppy says he doesn't keep his fish in a cage. So then Hers, of His 'n Hers, says, 'What about saying "unconfined" pets?' and then Tea-Cozy Head says that she would never *dream* of confining her budgie, Budjums . . ."

Aunt Barbie was wiping tears from her eyes and saying, "Stop! Stop! I hurt." Uncle Roger was snorting, and his face had turned bright pink with laughter. He blew his nose loudly. "What's this property they've got in mind?"

"It's one of those three-story brick apartments. I forget the name. Oh, hang on." Polly reached into her pocket and pulled out the flyer. "It's called Mowbray Court."

"Oh yeah, I've heard about this. Let's have a look." Uncle Roger reached over and took the flyer. "Don't tell me. Don't tell me. They want to preserve a quote unquote heritage building. The way people go on, you'd think these run-down old places were the Parthenon or something. Probably a perfectly good development site, and they want to keep it off the market. The Maxor Corporation has a perfectly good proposal. A real shot in the arm for business in that area. Whereas, co-ops! Where's the equity in that? Anyway, a year after these co-ops are set up, they're full of freeloaders, welfare mothers, the whole schmear."

"But, honey," Aunt Barbie's smile had evaporated, "some of those women . . ."

Uncle Roger talked right over the top of her. "But I don't think we need to worry. From Polly's description, it doesn't sound like those clowns could organize a garage sale, much less the purchase and renovation of a property. I somehow don't think Tea-Cozy Head represents a threat to the free market system." Roger rose heavily from his chair, winked at Polly, and headed toward the bar. Aunt Barbie held her glass out to him. Without looking at her, he took it, as smoothly as a relay racer accepting the baton. "Anyway, you seem to have your head screwed on right, Polly. Coke?"

"No, thanks." Polly felt a bit heavy and sick to her stomach. Maybe her period was on its way. Besides, she could feel the energy and warmth in the room seeping away, and she wanted to escape before it did. "I think I'll turn in now."

"Night, night, sweetie." Aunt Barbie waved her red-tipped finger in the air. Uncle Roger aimed his zapper at the TV, and as Polly closed the door, the manic laughter of a talk show audience welled up behind her.

10

Polly pulled a cleaning rag through the last piece of tubing from her horn and gave it a polish. She had done a thorough job this time, every inch of brass polished, all the moving parts oiled. The horn glowed like gold in the bright light of the bathroom. She slid the tube into place. Sticky. She needed some Vaseline. She searched through the bathroom cupboards. No luck. Maybe Aunt Barbie had some.

She walked up the stairs and pushed open the kitchen door. She heard Stephanie and Aunt Barbie talking in the family room.

"Have your invited Polly?"

"No, Mother. I haven't."

"Listen, Stephanie. We've been through this before. She's

your cousin and our guest. This time, either you invite her to come along or you don't get the car. Got it?"

"Yes, Mother, I've got it." Stephanie's loose-lipped voice dropped by one decibel. "Dictator."

Polly slid out the kitchen door and crept down to the basement again. She had barely pulled her chair up to the desk when Stephanie appeared and leaned in the doorway. "So. Do you want to come with me and Chelsea, or what?"

Something in Polly stiffened. Stephanie so obviously expected her to say no. Well, this time she wasn't going to be accommodating. For weeks she had been the "good guest," tidy, quiet, polite to Uncle Roger and Aunt Barbie. She had even been polite to Stephanie, who, when she wasn't ignoring her, treated her like some unwelcome and irritating virus. She was fed up with doing what people expected her to do. "Where are we going?"

"To a movie or something."

"Sure, I'll come."

Stephanie clicked her tongue in disgust. "We have to go, right now."

Polly stood up and picked up her jacket from the bed. "Okay, I'm ready."

"You might as well get in the back," said Stephanie as they went to the garage. "You'll have to, anyway, when we get to Chelsea's."

As they pulled out onto the street, Stephanie slipped a disc into the CD player, turned the volume up to high, and lit a cigarette. The windshield wipers cleared away a fine rain. The closed car vibrated to the beat of the music, and smoke swirled into the backseat.

Polly's eyes started to water. "Stephanie? Could you open your window a bit?"

"Oh, all right." Stephanie cracked open the driver's window. "I hope you're not one of those antismokers. They're so puerile."

Polly couldn't think of an answer, so she sat back in the soft, velvety seat and tried to type *antismoker* five times in a row on her knee in time to the music.

After a few minutes, they pulled into a driveway. Stephanie beeped the horn. A girl, dressed in black like Stephanie, appeared, with two boys following. The girl opened the car door and paused when she saw Polly. "What's this, kiddie night or something?"

"Um, this is my cousin," said Stephanie. "Polly—Chelsea, Brett, and Jordan."

Everybody mumbled hi, and Polly saw Stephanie lift her eyebrows and shrug at Chelsea as she slid into the front seat. The boys climbed into the back and Polly squeezed herself into a corner.

"What movie are we going to?" asked Polly.

"Movie?" Jordan snorted.

"Listen, Polly," said Stephanie, in tones of exaggerated patience, "we are not going to a movie, okay?"

"Then what *are* we doing?"

"Haven't you told her?" said Chelsea to Stephanie.

Jordan turned to Polly. "Let's just say that we're going to do some environmental cleanup."

"Yeah," said Chelsea, "we're sort of involved in waste management." They all laughed, and their laughter was like a wall, enclosing them and excluding Polly. She gave up and turned to look out the window.

"So, who's got a cleanup site in mind?" asked Stephanie.

"I've got one," said Brett. "Found it the other day. It's, like, totally welfare. Just head east, Steph."

Stephanie pulled out of the driveway.

"You won't believe this one," said Brett. "It's got everything—fake jade lions, a wooden wheelbarrow with flowers, and, wait for it, this is the best . . ."

"What?" said Chelsea in a high squeaky voice.

"Plywood butterflies!"

"Wow," said Jordan in awed tones. "This could be the best one yet. And definitely a job for . . ." He paused and then conducted with two hands as the whole group chorused, "Gross-busters."

Polly decided to storm the wall. "What's gross-busters?"

Stephanie exchanged a glance with Chelsea. "Better just tell her. Listen. You know all that bad taste stuff that people have around their houses? We hate it. So we do something about it."

"What kind of stuff?" asked Polly.

"I just told you. Things like birdbaths and sundials and . . ." The others joined in:

"Garden gnomes."

93

"Statues of saints."

"Painted rocks."

"Seashell-covered planters."

Polly interrupted. "But what do you do with them?"

A silence fell over the babble. "Let's just say," said Chelsea, "that we neutralize them. As a public service."

"Yeah. It's neighborhood enhancement," said Brett. They all laughed, and the walls went up again.

"I don't get it," said Polly.

"That's perfect," said Chelsea. "Keep on not getting it, little one."

"By the way," said Stephanie, "we're not particularly interested in other people knowing about this service, so I hope you're not going to be puerile about that."

"I guess we need the usual supplies," said Brett. "Pull over, Steph."

They stopped outside a small, run-down corner store. The sign, G. AND E. GROCERY, with its Coke medallion at either end, was peeling. Behind the steamed-up windows was a collection of huge houseplants.

"Who's going to buy the yogurt this time?"

"I will," said Chelsea.

There was a crackle of tension in the car, and Polly felt that understanding was being dangled just beyond her reach, like the spool and string games she played with Phoebe. What was all this about yogurt?

"Maybe we should send Polly," said Brett.

"Nah," said Stephanie. "I don't think this is Polly's thing."

I'm here. I'm sitting right here! Polly wanted to scream.

"Are we ready?" Stephanie clicked open the front door.

"Can I come in?" asked Polly.

Brett guffawed. "No, Polly Wolly Doodle, you can't."

The group piled out of the car and entered the store. Polly wiped the back window with her sleeve and peered out. The rain was heavier. She traced a single, light-filled drop as it slid slowly down the glass, gaining speed as it gathered other drops to it, and then racing quickly away. She blinked and refocused on the store interior.

At the back counter, an elderly man was sitting with a toddler on his lap. She saw Chelsea talk to him and the man turning around to the dairy case, the toddler balanced on his hip. There seemed to be a lot of back-and-forth conversation. She couldn't see the other three, although occasionally a shape moved in front of one of the partly obscured windows. Finally they all walked nonchalantly out of the store and got back in the car. As soon as the doors closed, however, Stephanie gunned the motor and they took off, with a squeal of tires.

Laughter and loud talk exploded as, one by one, they pulled things out from under their jackets. White glue and rolls of toilet paper, aerosol cans of whipping cream and shaving cream, cans of Coke. Chelsea took a small container of yogurt from the brown bag she carried. "This time I asked for boysenberry. That really confused him." She took off the lid and tasted it. "Yuck, what a gross flavor." She rolled down her window and threw it out. Polly craned her head around to see white, glommy yogurt spattered across the windshield of a parked car.

"Did you say that they've got a Saint Francis statue?" asked Jordan.

"Yeah."

Jordan held up the toilet paper and white glue. "How do you think it would look as a Saint Francis mummy?"

"Excellent!" The others shouted their approval.

Brett fingered the shaving cream. "And what about a little snow late in the season?"

"Hey, they'll be grateful," said Chelsea. "They're probably the types who spray fake snow onto their windows, anyway."

Polly looked at the debris littering the floor. "Did you guys steal this stuff?"

"We don't like to say 'steal,'" said Jordan. "We like to say 'liberated.'"

Polly thought of the discussions she had overheard at Vanessa's place about shoplifters in the hardware store. "I think that's a pretty jerky thing to do." Her voice cracked as she continued. "People who run small stores don't make very much money and they have to work all the time."

Chelsea spun around. "Oh, grow up, Polly. It's all covered by insurance. Nobody loses anything. Anyway, keep your Sunday school lessons for Sunday. Stephanie, did you have to bring her?"

Polly felt herself inflating with rage. "Yes! She did! Otherwise she wasn't allowed to borrow the car. But you've got

Pick-Up Sticks

the car so you don't need me anymore. Stop. I'm getting out."

"Shut up," said Stephanie. She pulled up to a red light and turned around, blowing smoke into the backseat. "Just sit there and shut up. Nobody wants to know your precious opinion." Stephanie had lost every trace of her English accent. She pulled away from the light with a jerk that sent Polly sprawling across Brett's lap.

Brett laughed. "Yeah, loosen up, kid."

Polly squeezed back into her corner. The windows were steamed over and there seemed to be no air in the car, only smoke. A clammy sweat broke out on her forehead. She typed *Brett* over and over again on the door. The distraction didn't work. Her stomach heaved. "Stephanie, I have to get out."

"Listen to Lady Macbeth. Cut the drama, Polly. You aren't going anywhere." Stephanie jerked the car angrily around a corner. Polly gulped to try to prevent the explosion and failed. Feeling her stomach rising, she scrambled into her jacket pocket for a Kleenex, but it was too crowded and she elbowed Brett in the face. Then she leaned over and threw up on the floor.

"Hey, watch where you're . . . Oh, jeez." Brett pulled his feet up onto the seat.

Chelsea wound down the window and rain gusted into the car. "Perfect. Great evening, Steph."

Stephanie pulled over to the curb. "Get out. What a pig. Chelsea, let her out your side."

Chelsea slid forward, tilting the seat with her. Polly crawled over the boys. Her foot caught in the seat belt and she half fell onto the sidewalk. The door slammed and the car spun away.

Polly threw up once more into the gutter, and then her stomach retreated and her head cleared. She took deep breaths of lovely, cold, wet air and found her Kleenex. Relief at her escape carried her through three deep breaths. But then, as she blinked the tears from her eyes and looked down the road at a single pair of taillights, the relief was replaced by a sense of abandonment laced with panic. Beside her ran a long chain-link fence, as far as she could see in both directions. On the other side of the street was a patchwork of rusting corrugated iron, padlocked gates, and concrete walls.

Nothing was familiar. No bus stops, no phone booths. She slipped her hands into her pockets. Alone, with one tattered Kleenex, a five-dollar bill, and a Chap Stick. A car hissed by and she stepped into the shadows. Get a plan. She couldn't just stand there. And there was no point going back the way they had come. It had been many minutes of Stephanie's fast driving since they had crossed any major streets. Better just to continue. She looked up at the smudgy lights on the north shore mountains to orient herself. Just walk east until she hit a street with a bus on it.

The rain fell harder. The slick road was pockmarked with drops and stained with patches of light from the streetlights. Polly pulled up the hood of her jacket and set off. She walked steadily, but the road seemed endless. The buildings changed. Warehouses were replaced by rows of dead-faced, closed businesses, with names that meant nothing—Basic Inquiry Studio, Filmon Industries, Cantech Consulting. Rain dripped off the bottom of her jacket, soaking the knees of her jeans and the tops of her running shoes. Soon she gave up looking ahead and concentrated on the sidewalk under her feet. "Step on a crack, break your mother's back. One, two, buckle my shoe. Three, four, shut the door. Five, six, pick-up sticks. . . ." She began to hum, enjoying the private sound reverberating inside her head.

Suddenly she was aware of something wrong. She was casting an elongated shadow onto the wet, shiny sidewalk in front of her. Where was the light coming from? Some instinct warned her not to turn around. Was that the sound of a car just behind her? She strained to hear, but her hair scratching against the inside of her hood masked the sound. She loosened the drawstring on the hood, and a rivulet of water ran over her face. Just over her left shoulder was the throb of an engine and the soft swish of tires.

All her body wanted to do was run, but she forced herself to slow her pace, willing the car to accelerate and drive past her. The car slowed as well. Her heart beat so loudly in her ears that she could barely hear. Without deciding to, she spun around and ripped her hood down. Headlights blinded her. Squinting, she could make out a bulky car shape and the movement of windshield wipers. And then a small sound, the click of a car door opening, exploded in her ears like a starter's gun, and like a sprinter, she was running.

Her feet slapped the sidewalk and she breathed in ragged gasps. She couldn't hear anything, but the light appeared to follow steadily behind her. Her legs felt heavy and slow, as though she was trying to run through water. A narrow opening between two buildings appeared and she jumped into it. It was dark and the ground was rough. Running one hand along a damp, greasy wall, she squeezed through a corridor to emerge into an area lined with loading bays. As she stepped out into the open, a spotlight flicked on. She held in a scream. For a second, she was paralyzed by the orange, humming light, and by a single brain-filling question: Who switched it on? Then she turned. Dodging boxes and Dumpsters she ran toward the darkness, straining to hear if anyone were following. Her foot slipped and she grabbed a garbage can to save herself. It teetered for a moment and then overturned. The lid rolled away with a clatter that echoed endlessly through the orange light. Under this sound, she thought she heard running footsteps.

She jumped toward a low wall, behind which was a slope covered in scrubby bushes. Her wet runners couldn't get a grip and she slid back, scraping her hands along the concrete. A sob was pushed out of her as she jumped again, this time scrambling to the top. The bushes grabbed her jeans as she pushed her way through them.

At the top of the slope was a jumble of wooden packing crates. Finally, a place to hide. She squeezed into one of them, wrapping the darkness around her like an old quilt. She tried to listen. All she could hear was her own gasps and the thrum of her heart pounding in her ears. But gradually her body quieted and she could hear the world again. A swish of distant traffic and the gentle hiss of rain. No footsteps. No crashing of bushes.

She took a deep breath and the sweetish smell of garbage wafted by her nose. The smell took her flying back to a hot summer evening in the backyard, the summer she was ten. She and Mum and Ernie and Mrs. Protheroe had been out for dinner, to celebrate Ernie's birthday. It had been the summer that Polly had begun her orthodontia and she was wearing a retainer. At the Pizza Palace she had taken it out and wrapped it in a napkin to set beside her plate. When they arrived home—no retainer. Mum didn't get one bit mad. She just phoned the restaurant. They said gloomily, "No, we didn't find it. But you can have the garbage."

So they went and brought home five giant black plastic garbage bags. Mum stopped at a corner store and bought three pairs of rubber gloves. And then she and Polly and Ernie knelt in the backyard and sorted through piles of Coke-sodden lettuce, cigarette butts coated in melted spumoni, tomato-stained napkins, and slimy pizza crusts. Phoebe kept dragging off bits of salami. Ernie got the giggles. Mrs. Protheroe dabbed them behind the ears with her lily-of-the-valley cologne, and Mum sang, "Oh, where is that appliance orthodontic" to the tunes of operatic arias.

And then, finally, at the bottom of bag four, they found it. For about a month after that, nobody, not even Ernie, was interested in pizza.

The distant clicking of a trolley bus brought Polly back to the present of her garbage-smelling crate. It was going to be hard to leave. The crate was safe and dry, a little house. But her grazed hand was starting to throb, her mouth tasted foul, and her wet feet were like ice. She unfolded herself and stood up. She would follow the sound of the bus. And she knew exactly which way was home.

CHAPTER

11

When Polly arrived at the warehouse, she felt she had been traveling for days. She paused for a few minutes to look up at the building. The mural of a cathedral painted on the side wall was reflected patchily in the street-lit puddles of the next-door parking lot. The rear end of a bicycle protruded from the bricks above the front door, the latest creation of the junk sculptor on the second floor. Polly held onto the last thread of taking care of herself and pushed the top buzzer, next to a card saying, CUSTOM LEADED GLASS. She leaned her face against the cool, smooth, painted door and waited.

A scrabbling sound from inside, the scrape of a dead bolt, and she was in Mum's arms. Moments later she was wrapped in an old tracksuit and sitting on the futon, propped up with pillows. Her hands were soaking in a bowl of warm water.

Mum crouched beside her and rested a hand on her knee. "What happened, Polly? Was it something at Roger and Barbie's?"

All Polly's thoughts and feelings tumbled and fell, like clothes in a dryer. All the loneliness of six weeks at Uncle Roger's crowded, empty house. Her fight with Vanessa. Missing Ernie. Hating Stephanie. And through it all, like the bright red pillowcase dancing among the other clothes in the dryer, the memory of what she had said to Mum. "Why did you choose to be a mother if you can't even do it right?" She shook her head.

Mum moved closer. "Polly, I have to know. You don't need to start at the beginning. Just jump in anywhere."

Polly pushed the words out. "I was behind this building and this big light went on. A big orange light. And I couldn't see who turned it on. I just ran."

"Where was this?"

"On some long street with lots of, like, warehouses. I was behind this building, with Dumpsters and stuff."

"It was probably one of those security lights. They're activated by movement. Nobody turns them on. But how did you end up there alone?"

With one thing explained, it became easier to talk. In muddled spurts Polly replayed the evening. "I couldn't stand to be in the car with them anymore. Then I threw up and they let me out."

"How come you were so unhappy? Were they just being mean to you?"

Don't tell. Don't be a fink. But why should she protect Stephanie? Who made up these rules, anyway? "No, they stole stuff from a corner store. They were going to use it to mess up people's yards and houses."

Mum was quiet for a moment. "I read in the paper about a rash of petty vandalism on the east side." She punched the futon. "And then they just left you? I'd like to wring Stephanie's neck. What a revolting little punk. And she's always had everything." Mum's eyes filled with tears. "Oh, Polly, I'm so lucky with you." She took Polly's hands and dried them gently on a towel. "I guess I should phone Barbie and let her know you're okay."

"Are you going to tell on Stephanie?"

"Well, I'm not going to get into it tonight, but I'll have to do something. Think of all the people with messed-up houses."

"I bet they didn't do it tonight. Not with a car full of throw-up."

Mum smiled. "True, but then there's the corner store."

"Oh, right."

Mum thought for a few minutes. "Look, I've got an idea. Do you think you could find the store again?"

"I think so."

"How much stuff do you think they stole?"

"Probably about twenty dollars' worth."

"Okay. I'll return the money to the store anonymously. Then I'll have a word with Stephanie. I'll tell her that I know the whole story, that I expect to be repaid, and that if I hear any news about further vandalism I'll spill the beans."

"That sounds a bit like blackmail."

"It's not like blackmail; it *is* blackmail, pure and simple. Probably not recommended in the books on child rearing, but who cares?"

"What about Roger and Barbie?"

"I'll let Stephanie deal with them. Does that sound okay?" Polly gave a jaw-cracking yawn and pulled her feet in under the covers. "Okay."

Mum tucked the comforter around her. "Polly? You don't need to decide this now, but, do you think you'll be staying here for a while?"

"For good," said Polly.

Mum smiled.

As Mum dialed, Polly felt herself drifting away. "Yes, I've got Polly here, safe and sound. Call me if Stephanie doesn't turn up. Otherwise, we'll talk tomorrow. . . . Yes, bye." Mum's voice came from a long distance. "Welcome home, Polly."

When Polly woke up the next morning, she couldn't remember where she was. Her nose told her first. The smells of linseed oil and coffee, the unmistakable studio combination. She rubbed the sleep out of her eyes and looked at the wall clock. Ten-thirty! She sat upright. The room was decorated with her clothes. Underwear, socks, and T-shirt, washed out, were pinned to the wall over the kiln. Jeans and jacket, the worst of the mud brushed off them, were hung from the overhead light.

On the door, impaled with a lead-cutting knife, was a note. She kicked off the covers and got out of bed to retrieve it. "You looked like you needed to sleep in. I've gone over to Mrs. Thing's to finish up cupboards. Breakfast in the blue bag on the counter. Back ASAP. See you then. Love, Mum."

She pulled on Mum's track pants and wandered around the room. Mum's tools on the wall, the bins of glass, the crumpled bed—everything looked crisp and sharp-edged, like the cut out bits of a collage. Her rainbow panel was propped in one of the large, high, bare windows. Sunlight streamed through it. She went to stand in the colored light, swaying back and forth, letting the rainbow colors kaleidoscope her scraped hands and bare feet. She turned around. The futon looked like the gym mats at school. She stepped back to the wall, took a run, and front-flipped over it. There was a thunder of applause and the judges held up their little cards. Every one a ten.

A rumbling in her stomach reminded her of breakfast. The blue bag contained juice, a muffin, and a banana. She turned on the radio and started to clear a space on the drawing table. A big brown envelope labeled CO-OP slid off

107

the top of a pile of papers and spilled a pile of newspaper clippings. Polly stuck a straw into her juice and started to browse through them.

"Developer Considers Mowbray Court," "Council Opposes Co-op Bid." She nibbled her muffin. " 'A very strong proposal,' said Alderman Blish at Wednesday's meeting, of Maxor's development scheme. 'Will give the district a shot in the arm.' " Another clipping showed a stony-faced woman: "Maxor spokesperson, responding to a question of Mowbray's heritage value, said, 'Well, we're not exactly talking about the Parthenon, are we?' "

The Parthenon? Where had she heard that before? Oh, yes. Polly felt a flush of shame as she remembered her conversation with Uncle Roger and Aunt Barbie after the co-op meeting. Uncle Roger must have read that article. What a copycat. She took one last slurp at the juice, dropped the box into the garbage, and pushed open the window beside her, sucking in the warm, sunny air.

"Not exactly the Parthenon." Suddenly she had a vision of all of them—Uncle Roger, Stephanie and her friends, all the developers and landlords and politicians—lined up, sleek and smug, know-it-alls, linking arms in one long line, calling out in mocking voices, "Red Rover, Red Rover, let *anyone* come over." And no matter how hard you ran at their line, you could never break through. Maybe if you ran in a big gang . . .

She began to stuff the clippings back into the envelope.

Something was in the way. She stuck her hand in and pulled out a button. It was decorated with sparkles and a picture of a fat-cheeked baby saying, "Save Mowbray Court." Tea-Cozy and her decoupage. Polly pinned the button on her sweatshirt.

There was a crash at the door. It opened, and Polly's suitcase came sliding in, followed by Mum's foot, followed by Mum with a box under each arm, a French-horn case hanging from two dead-white fingers, and a shopping bag in her teeth.

"Oof." Mum collapsed. "Tried to do it all in one trip. I was around by Roger's and I thought you could probably use a change of clothes."

Polly picked up the boxes and bags and arranged them in a corner. "What happened over there?"

"Not much. Roger was out. Stephanie was still asleep, and Barbie was on her way to work, but she suggested we have lunch sometime. I'm not holding my breath. I'll have my blackmailer's word with Stephanie, but I'll bet this is the last we hear of it. Anyway, are you okay? Did you get breakfast? How are your hands?"

"I'm fine," said Polly. "Would you like a cup of coffee?"

"Yum."

Mum took the mug from Polly and reached up to straighten the Mowbray Court button on her sweatshirt. She smiled. "I see you've found one of Gladys's buttons."

"Gladys?"

"I don't know if you remember her from the meeting. In her eighties? Wears this sort of toque thing? It always reminds me of a tea cozy."

Polly nodded.

"She's a real character. Since the co-op was organized, she's had a couple of chances to get into seniors' residences, but she's sticking with us because, she says, why would she want to live in a place with a bunch of old people? I really like her gumption."

"How are things going with the co-op plans?"

"We go to city hall next week and I think we have a chance. We have a good proposal, and a couple of city councilors are definitely supportive. Of course, anything could happen. We're hoping to dissuade Jason, that's the kid with the green hair, from speaking. He likes to refer to Maxor Corporation as 'that scum bucket full of scuzzbags.' "

Mum snorted into her coffee. "He has a way with words, bless his heart, but a certain lack of tact. Anyway, it's so amazing that we've come this far that I feel pretty hopeful." Mum paused. "I haven't been doing much apartment hunting, I'm afraid."

Polly smiled. "I figured."

"It's just that I'd hate to abandon this bunch now. I've grown so fond of them all. It's weird—at the last meeting we were having another long discussion on painting policy. Democracy is sure slow. Anyway, I tuned out and just looked around at everybody. And I thought, there's no reason why this should work. We're not related. We don't even have much in common. We're many of us a bit dotty. And then I remembered the paper-doll families that you used to make, cut out of catalogs. The sizes never matched. You had babies that were twice as big as dads. But it didn't matter. And the co-op group doesn't match, either. But it works somehow."

Mum shook her head. "But we probably should be looking for an apartment, just in case. We could go this afternoon. I've got Ludo's van for the rest of the day, and I'm more or less on schedule with Mrs. Thing's cupboards. We'd have to get a paper. . . ." Mum's voice trailed off and she ran her fingers through her hair.

Polly cleared her throat. "I've got another idea."

"What's that?"

"Why don't we drive out to see Ernie and Mrs. Protheroe?"

"Brilliant! A *much* better idea!" Mum jumped up, overturning her coffee. "A sunny Saturday, our own wheels, the call of the open road! I'll phone Mrs. P. right away."

Polly dug into one of the bags, looking for clean socks for her cold feet. She pulled out the face made of faces. It was slightly bent. Mouth, cheeks, chin, ears. There was a lot to finish. It was going to take hours, days. What a boring waste of time. What a waste of . . . taking care. She reached up to the design table, grabbed a pair of scissors, and cut an hourglass shape around the eyes. That was enough of a mask.

111

CHAPTER
12

Mum handed the can of Coke to Polly and fiddled with the radio. Music spilled out the open windows of the van, and a semitrailer roared by. Polly put her feet up on the dash and dipped into a bag of peanuts.

"This is great," said Mum, tapping a rhythm on the steering wheel. "I really feel like I'm on holiday. We should send postcards."

"Yeah," said Polly. Once on holiday, they had made a mission of finding ugly-sunset postcards from every place they'd visited. She had sent one every day to Vanessa.

Vanessa. She hadn't talked to her in three weeks. "Hey, Mum, could we really? Could we stop somewhere and get postcards?"

Pick-Up Sticks

"I don't know if they *have* postcards from the suburbs."

"It doesn't matter. Vancouver ones would do."

"Okay." Mum swung the van into the exit lane. "Bound to be a mall around here somewhere."

After some searching in the Valley Green Mini-Mall, they found a slightly dog-eared postcard of a killer whale breaching. They bought some Wite-Out and a fine felt-tip marker and Polly changed the caption to read, "Killer whale cavorts in Burnaby Lake." She filled in the message in her tiniest writing: "Having a lovely time. Shot the rapids in Burnaby River, rappeled down Burnaby Mountain, went big-game hunting on Burnaby Veld. Miss you. Wish you were here. Love, Polly."

They found a post office and Polly looked something up in the postal code book. Then they headed off again down the highway.

Even with Mrs. Protheroe's directions, a map, and two helpful gas stations, it was hard to find Sandringham Wynd. A maze of cul-de-sacs, all lined with townhouses and condominiums, nearly defeated them, but they finally found it—an eight-story building with pink and gold pillars. The front yard consisted of three sick-looking shrubs and a lawn of white, glinty, sharp-edged gravel.

"I'll bet Ernie just hates this," said Polly.

She pushed the intercom button and Mrs. P.'s voice crackled out. "Come in."

As they entered the lobby, the elevator opened and Ernie came out.

113

"I came down to meet you." He gave them each a hug, and then held his arms open wide, displaying a LIFE'S A BEACH sweatshirt.

"Pretty nice threads," said Mum. "Is that new?"

"Yup. Surfers wear them."

"Have you taken up surfing?"

Ernie giggled. "No, I'm too busy."

"What are you busy doing?"

Ernie pointed to the row of brass mailboxes that lined the front entrance. "I put mail in there."

"You do? Doesn't the mailman?"

"Our mailman's a lady. She lets me. Every morning I come down at eight-thirty. If she's late I just wait for her. She opens all these boxes with a key and she lets me put the mail in. And you know what? Every person here has the same postal code. Every single person! R. McAllister, one-oh-one; D. and D. Reilly, one-oh-two; Michael Maslin, one-oh-three; Occupant, one-oh-four . . ." Ernie ran his hand along the mailboxes and named all the residents.

"Ernie!" said Polly. "Have you learned to read since you got here?"

"No, I'm just good at remembering. But, Polly, you know what? You were right! Movie stars *do* live here. See this Victoria Roberts?" Ernie touched one mailbox reverently. "She's on television and everything. One day she had a parcel and I got to take it to her. She has a red sports car."

They went up in the elevator. "We go up to seven," said

114

Ernie. "There's *B* for basement. I have a secret there. I get to show you later."

Mrs. Protheroe met them at the door. She kissed Polly. Her cheek was as soft as an old pillowcase. "You've grown," she said, and they all laughed.

Polly did feel as though she'd grown as she edged her way through the crowded hall into the living room. Mrs. Protheroe hadn't disposed of any furniture, and it was all wedged into the small room. But then Phoebe *pirupped* at her ankles, and Mrs. Protheroe handed Polly tea in the special cup with birch trees, and everything was normal and familiar. Lace curtains hung in front of the peach-colored venetian blinds. The mantel above the gas fireplace was peopled with a line of china ladies. African violets dotted the many small tables, and the windows were crammed with every stained-glass sun catcher Mom had ever made for them.

Ernie sat beside Polly on the couch, and Phoebe jumped from one lap to the other, trying to be so charming that neither of them would ever stand up again. There was fruit bread and walnut squares and little sweet pancakes with jam. Ernie watched carefully as Polly drained the last drop from her teacup. "Are you finished yet?" he asked.

Mrs. Protheroe laughed. "Ernie's very anxious to show you something in the basement, Polly. But maybe she'd like another cup, Ernie."

"No, that's okay," said Polly. "Come on, Ern, let's go."

Sarah Ellis

When they got out at the basement, Ernie started bouncing up and down in excitement and chuckling. He led Polly around two corners to a heavy metal door, opened it, and flicked on the light. Lined along the wall of the small room were cardboard boxes.

"Ta-da!" said Ernie. "Know what it is?"

Polly shook her head.

"It's the recycling center," said Ernie. He began tipping up the boxes to show Polly what was inside. "We have brown bottles and green bottles and clear bottles. We have newspapers. We have cans. We have cardboard. Every day, after the mail, I go around all the floors with that cart." He pointed to a wagon in one corner, decorated with plastic flowers and decals. "I take all their stuff and I bring it here and wash the bottles if they're dirty and take the bottoms off the cans and then I squish them. I just step on them. Then I put them all in the right boxes. And when the boxes are full, Roy, he's Occupant one-oh-four, takes me in a truck to the recycling depot. I get to wear this hat." Ernie pulled a yellow plastic cap off the wall. "This is like what I used to do at V7R 1P2, but more. When I get home from work, Mum makes me lunch. Then I watch TV."

"Ernie, that's great! You're really helping the planet."

"The planet? Like Mars?"

"No, this planet, Earth. People who recycle always say, 'the planet.'"

"I'll remember," said Ernie.

"I've got something for you," said Polly, sliding a piece

116

of paper out of her pocket. "R2J 0K4."

"Neaters. What is it?"

"Manitoba Hog Marketing Board."

Ernie sighed with satisfaction. "Thanks, Polly. Can you come and live here? It's really nice."

"I don't think so, Ernie. But we came to visit, didn't we? And when we find somewhere to live, you can come and see us. We might go to live in an old apartment building with some other people. If we do, you could come and show us how to organize recycling. You could be a consultant."

"I could do that," said Ernie. "I could be a consultant."

When Polly and Mum left, Ernie came down in the elevator with them. He picked up some flyers that were dumped by the front door and piled them neatly in the lobby. Then he stood outside the apartment, on the gleaming white gravel, and waved good-bye.

The sun had set by the time they reached the highway. They drove along in silence for a while, a small darkness inside a larger darkness.

"You know what I miss the most about Ernie?" said Mum.

"What?"

"His singing."

"Me too," said Polly. "He must be the only living human being who knows the complete words to the theme song from "Gilligan's Island." The only one I could ever sing along to was "The Flintstones.""

"Hmm," said Mum. She drummed an introduction lightly on the dashboard. They both began to sing:
"Flintstones, meet the Flintstones,
They're a modern stone-age family. . . ."

CHAPTER

13

"Hunger gnaws at my vitals," Mum declared as they came back into town.

"But we just ate all that stuff at Ernie's."

"Hors d'oeuvres," said Mum. "What do you say? Shall we drop into Dot 'n Didi's for a burger before we call it a day?"

"Sure."

Dot did a double take as they came in the door of the café. "Bit early for breakfast, isn't it?"

"We're actually thinking more along the lines of a burger," said Mum.

"Excellent idea," said Dot. "It's a well documented fact

that hamburgers relieve dangerous pressure on the brain."

Mum and Polly slid into a booth.

Mum grinned sheepishly. "So, I guess my secret's out. I've been coming here quite often for breakfast. On my own I just didn't have the heart to get organized for cooking at the studio. Now that you're there, maybe we'll get one of those toaster oven things."

Dot leaned over the booth, pushed some paper napkins into the chrome holder, and poured Mum a cup of coffee. She flipped open the menu and read. "Do I understand that you would like the juicy satisfaction of one hundred percent beef, the chewy robustness of a sesame bun, the refreshing crunch of iceberg lettuce, the cheery sweetness of a rosy tomato slice, the unique medley of flavors and textures that define that heritage classic—the burger?"

Mum's mouth hung open. She grabbed the menu. "Dot! What's got into you?"

"It's Didi's nephew. You know the one who is having trouble finding himself? Well, he's taking creative writing, so he practices on our menu." She flipped open her waitress pad. "So—two unique medleys?" She looked at Polly. "Coke?"

Polly nodded.

Mum squooshed two creams into her coffee. "Heaven," she said. "Cappuccino bars come and go, but Dot 'n Didi's is eternal."

Polly looked around at the yellowing, dog-eared signs pinned to the walls:

Pick-Up Sticks

YOU DON'T HAVE TO BE CRAZY TO WORK HERE,
BUT IT HELPS.

EXCUSE THE DELAY,
WE'RE JUST HAVING A NERVOUS BREAKDOWN.

"I think I remember those signs from when I was a little kid."

Dot deposited their burgers on the table, giving each plate an elegant quarter turn to align it in front of them. "There we go. Special negative-calorie, cholesterol-free version. Better than oat bran."

They ate in concentrated silence for a few minutes.

"Yes," said Mum, "Dot and Didi keep things pretty much the same. You know, I've been coming here for seventeen or eighteen years. In a funny way, you were born here."

"What!" Polly dropped her pickle. She had a vision of Mum in labor over the lunch counter.

"Not literally, of course, but the *idea* of you. One morning Marcie and I . . . Do you remember Marcie? She was that red-haired dancer who used to have a studio on the third floor of the warehouse?"

"I think so."

"Well, anyway, one morning Marcie and I were in here eating pie and talking about babies. Seems like I was always in restaurants talking about babies in those days. I was telling her how I'd been looking into single parent adoption from another country, and how I was feeling pretty discouraged because it was so expensive and risky. Then Marcie

121

just said, out of the blue, "You could just have a baby, you know." And then we started talking about all the men we knew, and what we thought about their genes, and then we got a major giggle fit because it seemed so cheeky. And then we went on to talk about practical things—how I could take a baby to work and how Mrs. Protheroe would be a great step-grandmother and how Ernie would like to have a baby sister around. We had already decided that you would be a girl. And somehow, it just all seemed possible from that moment."

Polly moved her Coke glass around on the paper place mat, leaving a daisy pattern of wet rings. She felt Mum staring at her. She took a deep breath and pulled the red pillowcase out of the dryer. "Mum? Are you telling me this because of that stuff I said the night when I decided to go and stay at Uncle Roger's?"

Mum leaned over and tilted Polly's chin up. Her voice was thick. "I think you just got too smart for me."

". . . because I didn't mean it. I was just mad, and scared that we wouldn't ever find anywhere to live. Everything just got to me."

"I know that, Polly. I was pretty scared myself. But the thing is that sometimes you tell the truth when you're upset, or a piece of the truth that doesn't get said otherwise."

Mum paused as Dot refilled her coffee cup. Polly made a see-saw with her two plastic straws. She thought of pick-up sticks. You pull out one stick and the balance shifts and the whole pattern changes.

Mum continued. "What you said really rocked me because it reminded me of something that I had totally forgotten. It was that very morning, sitting here talking to Marcie. She said, 'What are you going to tell this child when she gets to be a teenager and accuses you of being selfish, of having her without a father around?' And I didn't know what to say. I knew I would just tell you the truth all along—that I wanted to be a mother but that I didn't want to be married. But about that question, the selfishness of it, I didn't have an answer. And it nearly stopped me. I wasn't sure if thirteen years would be long enough to figure out the answer to that one. I'm not sure it *has* been long enough. But then I remembered something else about that morning. I remembered just sitting here, looking around at everyone—at the sheet metal workers in their grubby overalls having coffee at the counter, at Dot and Didi with their pencils tucked behind their ears, at Marcie with her blueberry-colored teeth. They all looked so beautiful. Human beings seemed like the most wonderful invention." Mum turned to look out the window.

Polly studied her and saw, superimposed on the Mum of right now, a thirteen-years-younger Mum, eating pie, giggling with Marcie, finding the world suddenly beautiful. She realized that she had never put any energy into imagining Mum back then. She had used all her imaginings trying to visualize her father. She had made him up, again and again, handsome, rich, understanding, the father who never got older. And she would, no doubt, make him up again. She needed something to fill the father-shaped hole. But just at the moment, she didn't need him. He wasn't the point.

"Mum? You know about trying to figure out what to tell me at thirteen?"

Mum sighed and gave a twisty smile. "Yes."

"I think you just did."

Mum reached over and grabbed Polly's hand, and then they both discovered that paper napkins don't make good Kleenex. When Polly's vision cleared she glanced around the café. Dot had flipped the sign on the door to CLOSED and was sitting at the counter, wiping black gunk off the rims of the ketchup bottles. They were the last customers.

"Come on," said Polly. She slid out of the booth. "Let's go home."